I0645065

Tina had to be wrong. Otto couldn't kill any-one…could he?

Tina's eyes opened as wide as possible and danced between Otto and me, her jaw dropped, and her lower lip began quivering. I tried calming things down by just saying the first thing that came into my head to move the conversation along. "It feels so eerie, knowing someone did that—knowing they're out there somewhere." I knew as soon as the words left my mouth that it was the worst thing I could have said.

"That they could be coming for us," said Tina.

"Could be just one of those things," Otto said. "Someone lost control. Doesn't mean they'll do it again."

Tina's crazed look returned. She jumped up and sprang back. Once she was up against the wall, she leaned on one hand and grabbed a kitchen knife off the counter with the other. "Get out, Otto."

"What's wrong, Tina?" I asked, shocked.

"It's him. He did it," she shot back.

"W—what? N—no," Otto stammered.

But it was too late. She was convinced.

"Get out," she told him.

Otto tried to speak. "Tina—" he said but she quickly cut him off.

"Out!" she demanded.

It's Halloween night 1953, the last night of the carnival in rural Ohio, and a stripper turns up dead. Tom Davis, the chief of police, orders the carnies to stay in town while he investigates, but there are no leads to Mary's killer—no fingerprints on the murder weapon, no blood but Mary's at the scene, no foreign hairs or fibers—no clues of any kind. Brian Stockton, a reporter for the local paper, hopes this will be his break into the big time, so he begins to investigate as well. But, alas, the killer's identity eludes him, too. As tensions build, the carnies become paranoid, pointing fingers at each other. Could it be the owner, Bill Harris, the one who discovered the body? Or was it perhaps Gino Guglielmo, the man who runs the kootch show and has a nasty temper? Was it the eccentric clown, Otto Radowski, a man with dark secrets in his past and who just happens to have Mary's cat? And how did the killer manage to commit such a violent act without leaving a single speck of evidence? Mary certainly wasn't killed by a ghost…or was she?

KUDOS for *Death of a Kootch Show Girl*

In *Death of Kootch Show Girl* by Corey Recko, we are taken back to a small carnival in the early 1950s. It's a simpler time when the world was a safer place than it is today. But not much has changed when it comes to murder. When a striper in the carny's female revue is murdered, the cops do a cursory investigation, but when they can't come up with a suspect, they move on to other things. After all, it's just a dead striper. No big deal, right? But the carnies have other ideas. Right or wrong, they think they know who the guilty party is, and they want justice. The story is told from several different points of view, and the character development is superb. The mystery is intriguing with some surprising twists and turns. A really good read. ~ *Taylor Jones, Reviewer*

Death of a Kootch Show Girl is the story of a small carnival in 1953. The carnival plays in small towns in the Midwest through the spring, summer, and fall. But during their last show before winter break, one of the girls in the strip show is found dead, stabbed through the neck. The story, which is told from several points of view, follows the investigation through the eyes of the chief of police and a local investigative reporter, as well as several members of the carnival. When no clues are found and no suspects are identified, the cops shrug, but the carnies are enraged. They want justice and don't much care *how* they get it. *Death of a Kootch Show Girl* not only gives us a glimpse into the life of a carny, but it's also an interesting treatise on human nature. Plus it's an engaging mystery with a very surprising end. *~ Regan Murphy, Reviewer*

Corey Recko takes us back to rural America in 1953—a time when life was simple, bad things always happened to someone else, and the murder of a stripper was not worth expending the time or manpower to thoroughly investigate. But even strippers have friends, and when people are denied justice, the consequences can be devastating. *Death of a Kootch Show Girl* is a chilling tale told in a unique and refreshing voice. ~ Pepper O'Neal, author of the award-winning *Black Ops Chronicles* series

ACKNOWLEDGEMENTS

I'd like to thank the following people for providing valuable and detailed feedback about the manuscript: Sharon King-Booker, Diane Michaelsen, Trinisse Chanel, Joan Maze, Meg Recko, and the editors at Black Opal Books: Reyana, Faith, and Lauri Wellington. Thank you Duncan Eagleson for the terrific cover art, and to Jack at Black Opal for putting the cover together. I am truly grateful to all of you.

DEATH of a Kootch Show Girl

by Corey Recko

A Black Opal Books Publication

GENRE: MYSTERY-DETECTIVE/HISTORICAL THRILLER

This is a work of fiction. Names, places, characters and incidents are either the product of the author's imagination or are used fictitiously, and any resemblance to any actual persons, living or dead, businesses, organizations, events or locales is entirely coincidental. All trademarks, service marks, registered trademarks, and registered service marks are the property of their respective owners and are used herein for identification purposes only. The publisher does not have any control over or assume any responsibility for author or third-party websites or their contents.

To Meg, Gwen, and Hanna,
I love you

Chapter 1

Brian Stockton,
Saturday, October 31, 1953.

I took the first drag off my cigarette as I stepped onto the midway. I held the smoke in for a moment and felt a bit more relaxed as I exhaled. It was much more crowded than I had expected for a Halloween night. That didn't matter. Despite the lights and happy screams of children and adults alike, this old carnival was a depressing sight for me. There I was, just turned thirty and working for a small-town paper covering a shitty carnival—on its last night, no less. I didn't even know who I was writing for. What kind of person would want to read a review of a carnival after it was too late to go? But what the hell, it was a paycheck and all-expenses-paid night of second-rate entertainment, so I decided to make the best of it.

I strolled down the midway, passing food and drink stands. I saw a hot dog stand called "Ernie's Wieners" and began walking toward it when I noticed the "Geek" tent next to it. Ah, that carnival classic—the geek. The man who will eat live bugs, snakes, or whatever else for small change. Its bizarre placement next to the hot dog stand killed my appetite. I'd probably be unhappy knowing what was in any hot dog, but the thought of the geek's leftovers being so close worried me.

I took a right at the geek tent and walked down a stretch that included the "Hall of Mirrors," a "Test Your Strenght" game—yes, strength was misspelled—and some exhibit called "World of the Future." Since I knew what the hall of mirrors was, I decided to skip that and go straight to the "World of the Future." The wooden sign outside depicted spaceships, sleek aerodynamic cars, and the moon. It was apparently notable that the moon would still be there. I paid a dime and entered the tent.

Inside was a collection of low quality art and models depicting some vision of what transportation would be like in the coming decades. It took us from ten years in the future, decade by decade, to fifty years in the future, at which time, it predicted, we'd all have jet packs and be able to vacation on the moon. I might enjoy that if I'm still alive in 2003.

When I was back on the midway, I slowed as I approached a crowded intersection near "Dunk Bozo." That's when I first met that damn clown. Looking his way was my first mistake. I only glanced at him for a moment, but that was enough for him to notice me.

"Hey, buddy," he called out, "you in the black fedora and white shirt."

I stopped. That was my second mistake. He sat on a platform above a tank of water in a cage protected by chicken wire.

"Here at the carnival all alone?" he shouted at me.

"Yeah, so what?" I asked as I lit a cigarette.

"I just sees a lone man who doesn't appear to be very happy, and I says to myself 'he seems out of place.'"

"So?"

"Oh, nothing, nothing. Tell me, sir, what brings you here?"

I decided not to tell him that I was a reporter. "Nothing in particular."

"I bet I know what brings you here," Bozo said.

"And what would that be?"

"The girl show. Come on, fess up."

"So what if it does?"

"Oh, nothing, nothing. I just think it's pretty sad when a fairly attractive young man can't get no woman that ain't being paid to entertain him. But I suppose you got some reason."

I took a drag off my cigarette as this annoying man continued.

"You an alcoholic? A depressed drunk? I'll bet that's it. You look like a suicide waiting to happen. That's probably what keeps you from getting girls."

I knew what he was trying to do so I turned and left.

"Walking away from me and on to the girly show?" he continued. "That's alrighty, just don't kill yourself on the way over."

Was it that obvious that I was down on my life? I tried to forget about it—and about that damn Bozo. I had a story to write. I didn't need to spend all night trying to dunk some obnoxious clown.

I took a right off the midway after Bozo's tank. There wasn't far to go in this direction. The road or path, or whatever the hell you call it, ended at the Ferris wheel. I went toward the Ferris wheel, but didn't yet get that far. After only a few steps, across from the merry-go-round, an exhibit to my right caught my eye. The banner read, "Betty the Brainless Woman." Underneath the main banner was another sign that said, "Born Without a Brain!" The next show was in three minutes. I waited.

They let me into the Brainless Woman tent with two couples, one married and one younger couple that appeared to be on a date. Inside stood a doctor in a white coat with a stethoscope around his neck.

Betty was on a table behind him. She looked like a woman sleeping on her back. She was an attractive blonde who was about thirty years old. She had on a hospital gown.

Some wires protruded from under the gown and ran to a machine, which sat on the floor behind her head. It was about three feet high and had some dials on it.

The doctor gave a half grin that was higher on one side. "Welcome, one and all. I'm Doctor William Thomas, and behind me is Betty. Betty was born in a small Midwest hospital twenty-nine years ago last week. I worked at that hospital at the time. Betty's birth caused great panic throughout the hospital and the town. It was the biggest tragedy the town had ever seen. The tragedy was that Betty was born without a brain."

To my surprise, this "revelation" caused a few of the spectators to gasp.

"Betty's parents were, of course, horrified to hear of their daughter's terrible condition, but even more horrifying was the lack of sympathy they showed for their newborn daughter. They didn't care for her welfare or well-being at all. No. They were only worried about their own lives—about how the tragedy would affect them." He paused for a moment. "They hoped she would just die."

The twenty-something girl in the audience wiped the tear that ran down her cheek. Each of the four spectators I shared the tent with was visibly moved. I'm sure I looked concerned, too. Oh, I wasn't concerned about "poor" Betty. I was concerned that rational-appearing adults seemed to believe this cock-and-bull story.

"I knew then what I had to do," the doctor continued. "With the parents' blessing, I adopted Betty. I quit my job so I would have time to care for her. I devote twenty-four hours a day to her care. This show is our only income. Without the money we raise from attendees like yourselves, I wouldn't have the money to take care of Betty's medical needs. You make her life possible."

Holy Jesus. At that moment I heard a sniffle from the married man in the crowd, and his wife was crying. The doctor repeated his thanks then pointed to a jar where they could leave donations if they felt inclined. Even after their reactions, I was still shocked to see both couples leave money. I'd had enough of this and headed for the exit.

Next to Betty's tent was the supposed corpse of an Old West outlaw called Black Jack Elmer McCurdy. This I had to see. The carny that introduced the exhibit said the McCurdy was a train robber killed in the late nineteenth century. Law officers shot down McCurdy and, when his body went unclaimed, the undertaker decided to make some money with it by putting him on display. He'd been on display ever since.

McCurdy was dressed in western garb and had a six-shooter holster around his waist. His skin was brown and mummified. He wore a cowboy hat. My gut told me that the exhibit was yet another fake. Maybe not. How hard could it be for a carnival to get hold of a dead body? Still, I wasn't buying the Elmer McCurdy story.

Past the outlaw's tent was the Ferris wheel. I had no need to go there. I glanced at that and at the merry-go-round then turned back to the midway. I continued past the midway until I was in another section. I stopped and looked around. To my left was the "Museum of God's

Mistakes," with a sign underneath that expanded on the exhibit: "Human Oddities, Ten-in-One." To my right was the "Sword Swallower" tent, and straight ahead was the "Female Revue."

A midget barker stood on a platform next to a half-naked stripper, trying to convince the men that gathered around that the show was worth the price of admission. I was here to do a job, so I decided to hit the "Human Oddities" and the "Sword Swallower" first, and then I could spend some time at the revue.

The "Human Oddities" were in a dark, creepy tent, which was fitting. In the first booth was the bearded lady, which didn't interest me at all. After her was the half man-half woman. It was the third oddity that caught my eye. He was a man named Popeye. Although this middle-aged, dumpy man looked nothing like the cartoon sailor, he did wear a sailor suit and hat. Nothing appeared extraordinary about him, so I asked, "How does dressing like Popeye qualify you as an oddity?"

He said nothing. He just looked at me. Suddenly his eyes popped out of his head. The eyeballs were completely out of their socket and in front of his eyelids. He smiled.

I nodded. "Have a good night, Popeye," I said and walked on.

"You do the same, sir," the freak responded.

The next one was billed as the "World's Ugliest Man," and the billing may have been right. What a mutant. The man had no nose, just two holes in his face. He had a hair lip and two bucked-teeth that pointed virtually straight out. The rest of his teeth went in all kinds of directions. He definitely could have used a good orthodontist. But that wouldn't have fixed his other problems, not the nose, not the hair lip, not the, oh my God, I was still trying to deal with his teeth when I noticed the ear. Notice I didn't say ears. He had one normal looking ear, but the other one, his left one, was the biggest goddamned ear I had ever seen. It was almost as long as his head. And it was thick too! This isn't hyperbole. It looked like a two-inch thick piece of ham was stuck to the side of this poor man's head. I had to turn away. I couldn't take any more of that ear. I only hoped it wasn't real.

The next oddity was much more pleasing to the eyes. She was billed as "Tiger Girl." I'm not sure who they thought they'd fool with the stripes painted on her body and glued on whiskers, but this scantily clad tigress beauty was sure more fun to look at than that last of nature's mistakes.

After her was an armless, legless boy. The "Human Torso" wasn't much to look at so I passed him quickly. The "Cyclops" wasn't much better. He wasn't actually a Cyclops, with just one centered eye, but had three eyes. The third eye was in a canyon he had in his forehead. I thought the third eye was fake but the deformity seemed real.

"Wolfman" was next. His name described him well.

He was one hairy beast. After him was "Serpent Boy." I couldn't pass him up so quickly. He only wore a pair of small black shorts so he could show off his skin, which was covered in scales. He had no hands or feet. Each limb just tapered off like fins. I took my time studying this. If they faked this, it was damn good. I couldn't figure out how they'd do it. He looked at me but didn't say anything. I'm sure he knew that I was trying to figure out if that was his real body or just some horrible illusion.

The last oddity was billed as "The World's Fattest Woman." She was a wretched sight. She was a middle-aged woman in a two-piece swimsuit. The cottage cheese look of every inch of her body was undoubtedly real and extremely disgusting. The fat rolls completely covered the bottom half of the swimsuit that I could only assume she wore. She smiled at me. I felt sick to my stomach. How could somebody do this to themselves? I knew I wouldn't be eating for a while after seeing this mound of grotesque flesh. The worst part was the fans that were blowing on her. I'm sure she needed them to keep cool under all of that fat, but the odor they blew over from her smelled like dirty feet soaked in urine. I hurried away from that pile of blubber as fast as I could.

I exited the tent and just stood for a moment as I caught a breath of fresh air. Then I was on to the sword swallower—who, as his name suggests, swallowed swords. The country rubes seemed fascinated by him. The act did nothing for me. I was eager to get to the female revue if for no other reason than that I could sit down for a moment. I was sure the revue itself wouldn't hold any excitement for me. I already knew all about these kind of shows for reasons that need not be explained. Anyway, it was a second-rate carnival, and I expected second-rate strippers.

Outside of the tent, the girl used to draw the crowd in wasn't bad looking at all. Inside, the first stripper to perform in the packed tent was a haggard blonde who went by the unoriginal name of Juggs Mackenzie. She knew how to move, was obviously an experienced performer, and seemed not to mind the occasional call of "Grandma" from the crowd. She kept her bra on, probably because if she took it off her enormous breasts would hang to the floor. She had to be forty, minimum, and looked as if she had lived forty very rough years. The reaction of the mostly male audience was mixed, though she did make a few fans with her heated simulated sex against the tent pole. She reminded me of a Negro prostitute in Tulsa called "The Black Hole." The Hole looked as if she had been pretty once, too, but the years had not been kind to her either.

The next performer was the redhead I saw outside. Her large breasts were her biggest asset and she used them well, most impressively when she spun her tassels in opposite directions.

Following her a very pretty blonde girl took the stage. She was missing something the other girls had—legs. This legless beauty used her hands to walk around the stage. As she stripped, I didn't notice much because I couldn't take my eyes off of her pretty face and long blonde hair. Finally, I looked over her body. It was perfect—except for the lack of legs. She was missing the top heavy load that the previous two strippers carried, but what she did have looked much better. They were nicely shaped and very perky. She was in great shape. I couldn't find an ounce of fat on her. Whatever she was paid wasn't enough. I almost felt bad watching her perform naked in from of all of these men. When she finally did leave the stage, I decided it was time to go. At the exit I looked back to see an attractive twenty-something brunette take the stage. She had the cute girl-next-door look, and I was sure she would put on a hell of a show, but I was done with the kootch show for the night. I turned to walk out. Ah, what the hell? I decided to stay a little longer. There was something about that girl on stage. She was so cute that I couldn't bring myself to leave, so I stood at the back of the tent and watched. She put on a good show, but my eyes just stayed locked on her cute face. When she finished her performance, I left.

I made my way back to the midway. At the far end of the midway stood Devil's Lair. I bought a ticket. Devil's Lair was a car ride spooky house, with a satanic twist, which was obvious from the name. The exterior was devil red, black, and covered in flames. Inside it was divided into three sections. It began with a ride through a cemetery, which was followed by coffins and skeletons, and after that were the fire colors of Hell. It was cheaply made but had good character. It succeeded in creating a creepy atmosphere and was surely enjoyed by everyone who passed through its gates.

As I walked back down the midway, I saw a crowd watching as two carnies dragged an extremely obese man toward the exit. He was ranting about how he would "get that damn Bozo." Bozo was at his dunk tank, laughing hysterically.

I lit a cigarette and looked around the dwindling crowd as closing time approached. A light drizzle began to fall as I headed for the exit.

Chapter 2

Otto Radowski:

Ah, fried cheese on my break. It kept Otto going. I liked my job and liked it when everybody was looking and paying attention to me, old Otto, but I sure did love my cheese breaks. Oh well, back to work. Was time to let some asshole get his kicks by trying to dunk me in a tank. I knew how to pick 'em out good—to find the ones whose biggest thrill in life was putting someone else down—down in the tank in my case. Oh, I did love watching the frustration build when they couldn't dunk me. I had a good job.

I was sad it was the last night of the season. This Halloween night signaled the end of my working year. At seventy-two years old, it would seem old Otto needed the break, but that was not so. I got energy and life from my job. I did not want a break. I'd be here with my friends in the fun carnival atmosphere year round if it was up to me.

I entered the tank, got back into my seat, and looked over the marks. It was a big crowd tonight. Old Otto—I mean Bozo as I was in character—old Bozo thought he found his next mark.

"Hey, buddy, you in the black fedora and white shirt," I yelled to the man.

He did not appear to be enjoying the midway. The stuffed shirt looked at me.

"Here at the carnival all alone?" I shouted.

"Yeah, so what?" he answered.

Oh boy, I was reeling him in.

I questioned this unhappy man's reason for being here. He tried to cover his annoyance, but Bozo knew I was getting to him. We had a quick back and forth then I let loose the attack that old Bozo thought would bring him in. I was wrong. He turned and tramped away.

I continued trying to bait him, but it was no use. The man had more self-control than I thought. Oh well, there was a nice size crowd watching Bozo. I had plenty of people to choose from. I looked around until I spotted a young man about twenty, with slicked down hair, big glasses, and an awkward way about him. Bozo knew he had his next customer.

"Hey, four-eyes," I yelled. He glanced my way. I pointed to him. "Yeah, you buddy."

"Me?" he asked timidly.

"Yeah, you with the pimples. Why don't I see a girl by your side? None want to be with you?" I could see his face turn red with anger. Bozo done good.

"I'll have you know that I'm here with a girl. She's in the restroom."

"Hey, kid, your sister don't count." By the look on his face, I could tell I nailed that one. Oh boy, I had to laugh. I was reeling him in. He began to walk closer, but slowly. He paused between each step. "It's okay, son, some of us just don't have what it takes with the women," I said. "I bet you have lots of hobbies to keep you busy. No, don't tell me, let me guess. You collect stamps. I am right, ain't I?" His face was crimson as I hit another one. He now stomped over. I smiled. "You're not gonna try to dunk me, kid, are you? Come on now, you've probably never picked up a ball in your life."

That did it. He took out his wallet and put down a dime for three balls. "I'll show you," he told me as he shook his fist, which he made with the thumb on the inside.

He picked up the first ball and threw it wildly. It went about five feet too high and well to the left of the target. It was comically bad. I was glad he didn't show any ability. It was a cold night and I did not want to get wet.

Still, I let out a laugh at his pathetic throw to egg him on. I was enjoying myself.

He said nothing. He just turned beet red, picked up

another ball, and took a deep, long breath. He stared at the target, brought his arm back, and threw the ball almost directly into the ground. Ha! I said nothing, just laughed. I could tell that irked him the most.

"I'll show you," he exclaimed, his voice breaking.

He picked up his third ball. This time he wound up like a crippled girl softball pitcher, threw, and hit the chicken wire in front of me. Then the guy sprinted away. I think he may have been crying. That made me feel bad. This was all usually good fun, and the customer understood and enjoyed the game, with the exception of a man here and there who wanted to kill me. It pained me that I made him cry.

The crowd felt bad for him, too, and looked a little angry. I wanted to move on, but before I could pick out the next target, a big, athletic-looking man stepped up and bought three balls. He didn't need three. He dunked me with the first one. He then bought another set and dunked me again on the first pitch. He repeated this a third time.

The crowd enjoyed it, but it threw off my game. For the rest of the night, I had a hard time bringing in customers, and when Bozo did bring 'em in, they gave up after three balls. I even failed to bring in normally easy targets like feminine boys, weirdos, tomboys, and shorts. Before long, it was getting late, and our profits for the night were probably at an all-time low. Then I spotted the lard-ass that would save the night.

He was one of those big, sloppy assholes who probably ate twelve meals a day and got the food all over himself. This was a real glutton.

"Hey, tub-o," I called out to him.

He kept walking.

"Hey, fatty, I'm speaking to you."

That did it. He looked over. "Are you talking to
me?"

"No, I'm talking to all the other fat-asses around
here. Of course I'm talking to you. Anyone else here the
size of a Zeppelin?"

"Why you..." He trailed off as he stomped over.
"You can't talk to me like that."

"I think I can. In fact, I just did."

"I'll show you," he said to me, and then he asked
Leon, "How much are the balls?"

"Ten cents for three," Leon told him.

The man put down his money and picked up the first
ball. He gave me a cold stare.

I encouraged him. "Don't give yourself a heart attack. Throwing a ball is a lot of activity for someone of
your immense size."

He gritted his teeth and took slow, deliberate aim. He
threw and missed by a good foot.

I burst out laughing. "It's okay, tubby. That was a
nice try. Why don't you go home now?"

"Why don't you shut the hell up," he shot back.

He grabbed his next ball and quickly threw it. It was
out of control and missed by a few feet.

"Whoa, whoa, lard-butt, calm down. You'll never get me like that."

A large crowd gathered around. They were loving the exchange.

"Listen you," he said. It was clear that his emotions had taken over, which was good for me. "I've just about had enough."

"Well, if you dunk me, I'll stop. But I don't think you can dunk me."

The spectators loved the challenge.

"Oh, yeah," the genius retorted.

He grabbed his third ball then stopped. He stood still, intensely staring me down. Then he took a deep breath. He threw. Oh, it was close, much closer than I expected. He missed by maybe an inch. Typically as the marks get more emotional the throws get worse, but that damn near got me. He pumped his fist at the close miss and threw down a dime for three more balls. The man had a determined look in his eyes. He again took his time. His first throw of the new set was very close, again maybe missing by only an inch or two. That was as close as he would come. He became more frustrated, and his last two throws were far off. After his third throw, I yelled to him, "Come on porky, you can do better than that."

The comment worked. He bought three more balls as the crowd grew even larger. It felt good to have the crowd back after my earlier lull.

The big man missed by a lot with the next three

balls. After the last one, he let out a horrific scream. That's when the real fun began. The lard-ass climbed onto the counter—how it held his weight I do not know—and jumped toward my booth. Screaming like an animal, he grabbed the chicken wire.

"Come and get me, you disgusting pile of blubber," I taunted.

I couldn't control my laughter as this madman pulled wildly at the chicken wire. Spit was flying from his mouth and drool ran down his chin as he screamed at me.

The two carnies that grabbed hold of him had a hard time pulling him down. They were finally able to drag him away. He was kicking and screaming like a giant baby. The huge crowd watched, and I was ready for more business once I was able to stop laughing, but a light drizzle started and the crowd slowly dispersed. No matter, it was late and closing time was almost here, and, anyway, that man's tantrum was a great way to end the night and the season.

I waited a few minutes until the patrons were gone, then I left my post and walked through the drizzle as a few other carnies closed up shop. Only thing still open was the girl show. Most everyone was all ready to go home tomorrow. I'll admit it was a long summer. Still, I'd rather have kept going, but Otto would make the best of his break. I took time to walk the near empty midway, which was soon completely unoccupied. I made a circle around the carnival as I thought about the good times I'd had here. Soon Otto was soaking wet. I headed to the trailers. That was when I saw Mary.

It was a little while later when my boss screamed. "There's been a murder."

Chapter 3

Bill Harris:

It was finally the last fuckin' night o' the year. I had been waitin' fer this night fer a few weeks. I didn' generally min' my job, but by the en' o' the year, I was so damn sick o' the crowds, the kids, an' the smell. An' it was gittin' too cold fer my taste. I don't normally complain 'bout myself, but my knees was sore from all the fuckin' runnin' 'roun' I done lately. An' I was sick o' dealin' with all the little problems that come up. I was thrilled to think I was done fer a few months now. Tomorrow, I'd be packin' up an' I'd be in Florida fer the winter soon after.

The problems I have to deal with runnin' this carnival don't never stop, but it was close to closin' time an' nothin' was goin' wrong now, so when the drizzle started, I headed back to my trailer, spectin' to call it an early night, thinkin' everyone would close up an' that would be that. I wouldn' be needed anymore.

I made myself some hot coffee, added a bit o' brandy, put on a Glenn Miller seventy-eight, sat back, an' lit a cigar. It didn' git much better than this: the warm coffee, smooth brandy, soothin' cigar smell, good music, an' the crackle o' the old seventy-eight bitween songs mixed nicely with the rain outside. I was so relaxed that I had almost nodded off when there was a poundin' at the door. This pissed me off. I yelled, "Who the hell is it?"

"Open the door, Harris, it's important."

Shit, it was Gino Guglielmo. Gino had run the kootch show fer years an' had always been a bit o' a pill. He was wet an' aggravated when I answered.

"That bitch Mary was suppose' to give the last show."

"So?"

"So, she's nowhere to be found."

"Did you check her trailer?" I asked. It pissed me off that he was fuckin' botherin' me with this crap.

"Knocked and knocked. Nothing."

"So, what do you want me to do?"

"Fire her."

"I can't fire Mary. She's our bigges' titted girl," I explained.

He steamed in frustration until he finally said, "Well, do something."

"It's the last night o' the year. She probably got drunk an' passed out. I'll go talk to her," I told him.

"Well, okay," Gino huffed an' walked off.

This was all I needed. I let him make a few extra bucks by keepin' the girl show open after everythin' else was closed an' I was repaid by havin' to deal with this shit. I put down my cigar an' went out into the rain. Fire Busty? Was that greasy wop crazy? Busty Laroche was a huge attraction fer us. Sure, her girls were startin' to sag an' the years were becomin' visible on her face, but she was still a big draw. I was sure we could git another year out o' her, maybe more if she didn' min' the "grandma" jeers.

I knocked on her door but got no response. I had a key so I opened it up. I stepped in, but when I saw what I saw, I took step back. My heart dropped. I couldn' believe my eyes. Mary was face down in a bed full o' blood. I had to turn away. I looked again to make sure I saw what I saw, an' then I ran out o' the trailer. I tripped an' fell right into the mud, feein' it splash into my face. I got up, an' as I ran toward the midway, I yelled the shocking news. "There's been a murder!"

I ran to a pay phone at the front o' the fairgrounds to call the police. I saw Adrian as I was runnin' to the phone so I stopped. All o' the stress made me hungry so I asked Adrian to make me a burger. I called the police, went back to Adrian's stand to git my food, then wen' to the backyard because everybody was outside. I reckoned that the police wouldn' want a crowd so I asked everyone to return to their trailers. I went to the entrance an' waited fer the police to arrive. I was eatin' the burger as I saw the police car pull up with one man inside. He got out an' came toward me. I hel' out my han' to him. "I'm Bill. I own the carnival."

"Chief Davis," he responded.

"It's this way," I said an' took him to the scene. "She's in there."

He went in an' looked around. He then came out, talked to his deputy for a few moments, then asked me to introduce him to everyone who werked fer me. We moved at a hectic pace as I introduced him to every carny, an' he looked in every trailer but one. It was when we knocked at Gino's door that we had trouble.

"Yeah, Harris, what do you want?" Gino asked when he answered.

Chief Davis responded before I could. "I'd like to ask you a few questions and take a quick look inside your trailer," Davis stated.

Gino looked at me then back at Chief an' said, "You can ask me whatever you want, but you can't come in here."

"May I ask why I can't come in?"

"It's my fucking home and you don't have a warrant. I know my fucking rights. You need a warrant to enter. Now, if I let that go, I might as well be your fucking slave. You can have your way with me and fuck me on Sundays or whatever sick shit you're into."

What the fuck was that crazy dago doing? If it was me, I would have arrested him right there, but the copper kept his cool.

"I won't look inside then," he said to Gino. "What is your name, sir?"

"Gino Guglielmo."

"When did you last see the victim?"

"Earlier in the night for her last show. She was suppose' to do another but never showed."

"Did you see anything suspicious?"

"Nothing."

"Thank you. That will be all for now," Davis said an' moved on. "To the next one," he said to me an' we continued to visit my werkers until we had seen 'em all. Then we went back to Mary's trailer so he could have another look. "If you want to go to your own place to stay dry, feel free," he told me. "I can come to you when I'm done here."

"I'll do that," I said an' walked off.

I normally didn' mind the chilly an' wet weather, but my joints were achin' in this cold rain.

Inside I dried off, sat down, an' tried to collect my thoughts. I felt sick over what happened to Mary, an' angry that it could have been done by one o' my people. After a bit o' time there was a knock. It was Chief Davis. I invited him in an' we sat at the front part o' my trailer, which held the office pertion where I conducted all o' my business. He sat in a chair facin' my desk an' I sat behin' my desk. I offered him a cigarette. He accepted it an' commented on my expensive cigarette case.

"French case?" he asked.

"Good eye," I said to him. "I picked it up durin' the Great War."

"I fought in the second," he said.

That gave me more confidence in him. I wanted to tell him this but before I could he asked me my full name an' then what I was doin' until I discovered the body. I told him 'bout the night right up to findin' the body, but when I got to tellin' him ''bout what I found, I couldn' finish the sentence as I thought 'bout what I had seen.

He asked me how long I owned the carnival an' how I started the business. I told him my backstory: my days as a cook savin' money an' goin' into business fer my-self, my vision o' the carnival, an' a brief rundown o' my last fourteen years. Then he asked me how I met Mary an' 'bout my relationship with her. It was difficult to talk 'bout her. It hurt bad.

He followed this by askin', "Do you know of anyone who might have wanted her dead?"

I thought over what I should tell him. I wanted to help but didn' want to make it soun' like she was in any way to blame. As I was thinkin', he rephrased the ques-tion. "Can you think of anyone that might have done this?" I took a long breath as I thought. "I can't solve this if you don't tell me everything," he told me.

"Well, I don't want to make her soun' like a bad person er nothin'," I said, an' continued with what I didn' want to say.

Chapter 4

Tom Davis:

I planned on a late night, it being Halloween and all. I had my Deputy-Chief, Paul Inzalaco, hang around the station for any calls that might come in while three other men and I patrolled the town—me and one other by car and two on foot.

It turned out to be a quiet night. I hadn't expected much—this was a quiet town where there was never serious trouble—just a Halloween prank or two that went too far. On my patrol, I didn't come across a thing, with the exception of a speeder as I was heading back to the station.

When I returned, I found Paul reading *Life* magazine at my desk. He looked up as I entered. "Anything to report?" I asked.

"Not a call all night."

"I didn't come across any trouble either. Why don't you take off?"

"All right." Paul stood and grabbed his coat. "You coming?"

"I have some paperwork I've been putting off. I'm going to take care of that first."

"Okay. Bye, Tom. See you tomorrow."

"Bye."

Paul left and I sat down at my desk. The work took me just over an hour. I was finishing up when the phone rang. Normally a call at this time of night meant a minor problem with some juvenile delinquents, but not this time.

A carny was murdered. I was sorry to hear that. Most people didn't give a damn about carnies, but I had a soft spot for them. For a summer after high school, I was one. I was a geek. I'd eat anything back then.

I phoned the county sheriff's office to inform them what had happened. Then I called Harvey Watterson, who was on patrol, and asked him to come back to the station to sit by the phone. I called Paul—he was just about to go to sleep—told him to meet me at the fairgrounds, and then I left.

So there I was, driving down a dark road on a rainy night to the fairgrounds. It was a quarter past midnight and I really wanted to be home, but I had a job to do.

When I arrived a dirty, fat man with coffee stains on

his shirt met me at the entrance. He had a hamburger in one hand and held out his other. "I'm Bill," he said. "I own the carnival."

"Chief Davis," I responded as I shook his greasy hand. The rain was falling and it was cold. If it were a few degrees colder, it would have been snowing.

"It's this way," Bill said as he led me to the back-yard. The ground was muddy. The big carny stepped hard as he led me to the crime scene, splashing mud on me with each step. The victim's trailer was in the farthest corner of the backyard. The door hung open.

"She's in there," Bill told me.

I went in. As I entered, my first instinct was to look away. The scene was not pleasant. The victim was nude. She was in her bed, face down. A large knife was under her, stuck deep in her head. It entered at the uppermost portion of her neck at the back of her jaw. Her head was hunched over the handle. What appeared to have once been white sheets were stained red with blood. I took a quick look around. Nothing suspicious caught my eye. I exited the trailer.

I was hoping my deputy would arrive soon, even though, despite him being a good guy, I knew he wouldn't be very helpful on a case like this. I wasn't sure if anyone on my force would be. We didn't have trained detectives. I had been one for a few years but that was a long time ago. We were a small town, so we didn't have many resources. I fully expected that a detective sent out by the county sheriff would take the lead in this case and that we would just support him, but until he arrived, I was in charge.

I decided that, in the morning, I would call Cleveland to get the coroner there to help our local coroner. Old Gus Walker was competent enough, but we didn't have murders here…well, not like this anyway, and I knew Gus wouldn't be able to provide much help. For now, I was on my own. Then I saw Paul walking up. "Paul," I said to him.

"What happened?"

"Murder."

"Oh, wow. I'm here for you. What do you want me to do?"

"Go stand out front. Someone from county should be coming by. Point them in this direction."

"Got it. Then what?"

"Head back to the station. I'll need everyone in early tomorrow. Arrange that, then stay by the phones and send Harvey back out on patrol. Have him do a quick drive through town. Once he checks everything out and returns, he can stay with the phones while you get some sleep."

"But—"

I knew what he was going to say.

"—don't you need me to help question witnesses?"

"The most important thing you can do now is just what I asked. If the killer left here covered in blood, someone may have seen him and called the station. Harvey may have gotten a call already. If a call comes in, check it out."

"Yes, sir," he said.

He never called me sir. He even saluted me then turned around and walked toward the entrance. My mind turned back to what I needed to do here.

I suspected that someone involved with the carnival was responsible for this girl's death, but who? I needed to speak with everyone, one by one, that night, while the crime was fresh. And I needed to check everybody immediately. Maybe the killer still had blood on him.

"Bill," I called out. "I want to be introduced to every carny you have, immediately. No time for small talk. I need to see everyone, and need to see inside every trailer, now. Somebody on this lot has that girl's blood on their hands, and I intend to find them."

Bill led me from trailer to trailer as fast as we could go. I didn't have time for small talk or to conduct interviews. I just wanted a quick look at everyone and every trailer. I did not have a warrant, but most everyone was cooperative. Only one man, Gino Guglielmo, refused to let me in without a warrant. He was very clear about his position so I saw nothing to be gained from arguing. Besides, I did manage a quick glance inside and did not see any blood on him or in the trailer. The quick search of the carnies and their trailers didn't produce any evidence. If the guilty party was here, they somehow already cleaned up. The rain may have helped.

I went back and stuck my head in the victim's trailer. I didn't see any signs of anything. The blood was confined to the bed area. Was it possible that the murderer left the crime scene blood free? This would make things more difficult, but I couldn't deal with that now. Men from county would investigate that.

As I stepped down from the trailer, one of those men greeted me. "Chief Davis?" he asked.

"Yes, I'm Tom Davis."

"Detective Pat Perry." He motioned to a man on his left. "This is Roger Poole, the medical examiner." Then he gestured toward the man to the left of Poole. "That's Lynn Nolan. He's from the lab," and, as Nolan nodded, Perry motioned to a woman on his right. "And Lori Kirk is the photographer."

Poole was carrying a small black bag, Nolan had a large box with a handle in one hand and a vacuum in the other, and Kirk held a dark-brown leather-covered box by its handle.

"We'll check out the scene," Perry told me.

"Go ahead," I said as I stepped aside.

They went in. It couldn't have been more than five minutes when Perry stepped out.

"Davis," he said.

"Yes?"

"Poole estimates the time of death was within the last hour and a half. There is no swelling so we know she died quickly. He'll put together a full report after the body has been fully examined by him and the county coroner. Nolan will bag the weapon and take that, and anything else that he feels needs microscopic examination, back to the lab. He's going over the room with a magnifying glass now. He'll check for fingerprints and then will run a vacuum sweeper over the entire room to see what turns up. There were no mud or dirt footprints. Maybe the killer was smart enough to take his shoes off outside." Perry smiled, as if he intended this last statement to be a joke, and then continued, "When the reports are complete, they will be sent directly to me and copies will be made for you. You can take it from there."

I was more than a bit surprised. "Excuse me?"

"Take care of it. There's nothing I can do that you can't."

"I don't have much experience with these types of crimes. I haven't investigated a murder in years," I protested.

"Listen," he said. "So far we're not finding any evidence here that would lead to a suspect. There ain't nothing here, but if the lab report does turn up something, you'll know what to do with it."

"You're the detective."

"Look, Davis, the sheriff ordered me not to spend any extra time on this unless it was absolutely necessary. It was just a stripper that was killed. It isn't like we lost some upstanding member of society. She isn't even a local."

I couldn't believe what I was hearing. "She was a human being."

"We have limited resources and have to prioritize. She isn't a priority."

"What about the murderer on the loose?"

"We both know that murderer will probably be leaving town when this carnival packs up and goes. If you can find him before that, great, if not, it isn't our problem."

"So that's it? You're done?"

"No, not done. As I told you, you will get reports from both Poole and Nolan, and I will have a look at both. Photographs of the scene will be taken. Any interviews you conduct, send the transcripts downtown, and I can look them over as well. I'm here for you if you find anything."

He sickened me.

"All right, I'll get on the investigation." What else could I say or do?

"Sounds good. We'll finish up here. Why don't you speak with the carnival people?"

"Fine," I said. So it was up to me.

First, I needed to interview everyone here, tonight. I decided to start with Bill.

Chapter 5

Arianna Lewis:

I was looking forward to returning to Kansas for the winter, seeing my family, and relaxing in familiar surroundings. Though I enjoyed going to different places, I was ready for a break from the travel and work. Not that my job was that difficult. Stripping is easy if you are comfortable with it. Sure, it's not for most folks, but I'm not most folks. I don't have any hang-ups about nudity. It wouldn't be my first choice for a job, and I certainly wouldn't say I liked taking my clothes off for strangers, but I have no huge problem with it. I wouldn't enjoy working as a waitress either. It was tough getting used to, since offstage I am quite shy. But after doing this a while, I reached the point where I felt powerful and confident onstage—when I was in the right frame of mind anyway.

Sure, sometimes being out there is depressing. There are creeps in each town, and they make the job especially difficult. Fortunately, the majority of the men are quite respectful.

It was when I wasn't performing that I loved what I did. The job offered me the opportunity to travel throughout the Midwest and East. Before this, I hadn't gone much more than one hundred miles from my small town. The most exotic place I had visited was Tulsa. This job also gave me the chance to make many great friends among my fellow carnies. I was certain I'd stay in contact with some of them for the rest of my life.

It was with mixed emotions that I finished my final show of the year. I didn't know if I'd be back again. I enjoyed the travel and my many friends, but I didn't want to spend my life on the road. I wanted a husband, children, and, I know people thought I was foolish for saying this—a career. I wanted something I could do each day that I was proud of doing. I wanted to be a productive member of society. But I put all of this out of my mind as I stepped in front of the audience, perhaps for the last time.

I confidently strode to the center of the stage. I was wearing a lacy black bra and frilly black panties. I smiled, winked at a random gentleman in the audience, and began gracefully sliding my hands down my body until I reached my ankles. I sprang up and began my upbeat but sensual dance routine, making eye contact with different patrons as I danced. I gave this final performance of the year—and maybe ever—my all. I tried to enjoy it, but this disturbing guy in the front row was everything I hated about this job. It would be fine except for men like him. His face was like stone, as if stiff from anger—an angry lust. The look was unnatural. It sent chills down my spine. It wasn't simple attraction or lust. There was something violent about it. Every few nights there was a man like him. It was just something I had to deal with. I tried looking at everyone but him. His presence made me feel very uncomfortable as I removed my top, under which I had on only very small pink pasties. I made eye contact with a conservative looking man in the second row as I slid my hands up to my breasts. I smiled at him then strutted around the stage, shaking all I had.

As I neared the end of my performance I turned my back to the audience, put the creep out of my mind, and slowly ran my hands down my legs as I bent over to hoots, hollers, and cheers. I looked at the audience from between my legs, winked, then stood up and departed the stage with a smile. As soon as I was off the stage, I felt exhausted.

At that moment, Gino stormed out of the back, incensed and yelling something about going to get "that bitch."

I thought about asking someone what was going on but I didn't care enough. It wasn't important and I didn't want the drama tonight. I threw on my sweatpants and sweatshirt. I took a moment and looked around, wondering if I'd ever see the inside of this tent again. Then I exited into the cold night.

I walked on the outside of the midway, behind the stands and exhibits, and looked between them, at all of the people and lights, and listened to the sound of the crowd. A light drizzle began to fall, which just added to the emotion of possibly closing this chapter of my life. I hadn't made the decision not to come back yet for certain. There was still the possibility I might give it one more year. Being on the road had been everything I had hoped for and more. I just felt that I had probably gotten everything out of it that I could, and I wanted to try so many other things in my life. Now, perhaps after these experiences, I would have the courage to do everything I wanted. I looked out on the lights of the Ferris wheel and smiled as I felt the excitement of the carnival.

Then, as I walked back to my trailer, I became sad again. Whether to come back for one more year or not was a difficult decision. I could already feel the heaviness on my heart as the question loomed. In the morning, I would say good-bye to everyone, many of them possibly for the last time. I'd miss the carnival. I wanted to cry.

I sat alone in my trailer and thought back on the summer and about my friends. There were tears in my eyes and an empty feeling in my bosom. I was in this emotional state when I heard Bill scream, "There's been a murder."

The scene was chaotic as everyone rushed outside. Bill asked everyone to return to their trailers while he went and waited for the police. I understood why he made the request, but it wasn't that easy. Who wanted to be alone right now? We were shocked and afraid. We all huddled in small groups. I stood with friends Otto and Tina in the cold rain. We weren't talking but the company helped. Bill was right, we should all have been inside, so I invited them to come in my trailer so none of us had to be alone.

To my invitation Tina quietly responded "Okay" and Otto simply nodded.

I was cold, so as soon as we entered I walked over to make some coffee. I asked if they wanted some, and they both accepted. After starting it, I leaned on the counter and stood facing them. The silence was uncomfortable, and I was glad when Otto broke it.

"Oh, lordy, poor Mary," he said.

Tina looked like she was ready to cry. "Yes," she said. "She was such a good person. The kind of person who never hurt anyone." While she thought of Mary, she smiled. "I once saw her putting a spider out from her trailer because she didn't want to harm it."

"That sounds like Mary, always thinking of others, human or animal," I said, and following a pause added, "or spider."

Suddenly, Tina's smile turned down and her mouth opened slightly as her expression turned back to worry.

"My God, what about her cat?"

"I don't know," I said as I began pouring the coffee. It was an important question. The poor cat couldn't just be left there with her dead body.

"I have Roscoe," Otto finally said.

"You?" Tina asked. "Why?"

"I'm not sure," he responded. "Earlier tonight, just as we was closing, Mary asked me to watch him for a while. Said she'd be back soon to get him."

"That's strange," I said as I brought the coffee to them. I sat down. "I wonder why she needed you to watch Roscoe."

"I don't know," he replied. We sat silently and drank. The rain outside was the only sound for a while.

"Well, she is in a better place now," Otto said, breaking the silence.

Tina suddenly became excited. "Excuse me?"

"A better place. You know, Heaven."

Tina's eyes opened as wide as possible and danced between Otto and me, her jaw dropped, and her lower lip began quivering. I tried calming things down by just saying the first thing that came into my head to move the conversation along. "It feels so eerie, knowing someone did that—knowing they're out there somewhere." I knew as soon as the words left my mouth that it was the worst thing I could have said.

"That they could be coming for us," said Tina.

"Could be just one of those things," Otto said.

"Someone lost control. Doesn't mean they'll do it again."

Tina's crazed look returned. She jumped up and sprang back. Once she was up against the wall, she leaned on one hand and grabbed a kitchen knife off the counter with the other. "Get out, Otto." she said forcefully.

"What's wrong, Tina?" I asked, shocked.

"It's him. He did it," she shot back.

"W—what? N—no," Otto stammered.

But it was too late. She was convinced.

"Get out," she told him.

Otto tried to speak. "Tina—" he said but she quickly cut him off.

"Out!" she demanded.

"Mary was my friend," Otto said.

I knew it was useless, but I wanted to calm her nerves and stop this overreaction. "Tina—" I said. I was able to say no more.

Tina ignored me completely. "Out! Out! Out!" she shrieked.

I looked at Otto. "You better leave."

I didn't want to throw him out, but had no choice. I gave him a sympathetic look and hoped he understood. I couldn't imagine how the poor guy felt, being accused of such a heinous act. He started to speak, but then seemed to understand the situation, and left. I felt horrible having him leave but it couldn't be helped. I wanted to try talking to Tina and ease her concerns, but now was not the time. She was crying hysterically and needed comfort, nothing more. I moved close and put my arm around her. I held her for I don't know how long.

She had barely calmed down when there was a knock at the door, which made her shriek.

"Who is it?" I called out.

"Police."

"Just a moment." I walked over and opened the door. A policeman stood there.

"May I come in?" he asked. "I'd like to ask you some questions."

"Yes, please."

He entered. He nodded hello to Tina. "I'd like to speak to each of you alone," he said.

Tina's eyes grew wide.

"Is that necessary?" I asked. "My friend, she shouldn't be alone right now."

"I'm afraid it is," he said sympathetically. He looked at Tina then back at me. "I promise to make it quick."

"Well—"

"It's fine," Tina interrupted. "I'll step outside."

"Thank you," said the officer.

Tina put on her coat, got up on her hands, and left.

The police officer introduced himself as Chief Davis and sat down. He looked to be in his mid-thirties and bore a striking resemblance to Errol Flynn, even down to the pencil-thin mustache, though he was ever-so-slightly heavier than Flynn was at that age. He started by asking me if I knew of any enemies Mary had. Then he asked if I knew of anyone who might want her dead. I instantly thought of the victims of her hotel room key scam. I often warned her that selling bogus hotel room keys to strangers was a bad idea, but she always just laughed it off.

"Well," I said, "there's this one thing she did. When—" At that moment I paused as my brain momentarily locked. It was probably brought on by the stress of the night. I gathered my thoughts and explained the scheme to him.

He asked me whether she sold any keys that night or invited anyone back with the intention of conning them, but all I could tell him was that I did not know of her doing anything like that.

"Do you know of anyone associated with the carnival that might want her dead or have any motive to kill her?"

This was a difficult question to think about. I had friends here, and it was hellish to think about any of them doing anything like this, but I took the time to search my mind for any possible motive someone may have had.

After some thought, I answered, "No."

He then asked me about that night, from earlier during the show to when I heard the cry of, "There's been a murder," from Bill. I didn't want to think about any of this, but knew I had to. I answered the questions as best as I could. That was it. He had kept his promise. It was a brief interview. I stepped outside and Tina stepped in.

I hated standing outside alone in the rain. I could see Mary's trailer. Knowing what was done in there, that her body was still inside, and that the person who did it was out there somewhere, was a horrible feeling. Tina was with Chief Davis longer than I was, and it seemed like forever.

After standing there for longer than I had expected, I heard a bang that sounded like something hitting metal. My heart sank and I immediately reached for the trailer door. I looked in the direction of the noise. I did not see anything out of the ordinary, nor did I hear anything suspicious. I moved away from the trailer and took another step toward where the noise came from. I still saw nothing. I knew the wind had probably just blown something into the side of a neighboring trailer. Still, I was scared.

It was a great relief to me when the door opened and Davis stepped out. "All done," he said.

"Thank you," I said and went inside.

Chapter 6

Otto Radowski:

Oh, what a night it been. After the cry of murder, everyone filled the backyard around the trailer. Bill asked us to clear out, said the cops were coming and wouldn't want a crowd. Okay, okay, I thought. I cleared out. We all did. All backed off so there wasn't a crowd in front of Mary's trailer. Some people went inside while others gathered in other spots. Everybody would soon go indoors because of the rain, but at this moment, some people needed to talk or didn't know what to do. Mary's death had shocked us all. Poor Mary. So bad, she had to die. Made me sad. She been nice to me. She done things to me no one else ever did. She liked Otto and Otto liked her.

Everyone was uneasy. We all scared. I got to talking

with Arianna and Tina. Arianna invited both of us back to her trailer 'cause she didn't want to be alone but didn't want to keep standing in the mud and rain.

We were wet and cold when we got inside. Otto was shaking a little. I felt a nervousness after all that happened. Arianna put on some coffee while Tina and I sat down and talked about poor Mary. Talked about the good person she was.

They got to worrying about Mary's pussy but I put their minds at ease. For a bit, we sat in silence. I sipped the coffee. It warmed me up and calmed me down. I noticed Tina seemed to be staring at old Otto. She was a beautiful girl, except for the no-legs thing. Slender body, small but shapely breasts, long blonde hair. I watched her show a few times from the back of the room, I confess.

The only noise was the heavy rain falling outside. I didn't like the silence so I said, "Well, she is in a better place now."

Arianna sat silent, but Tina exclaimed, "Excuse me?"

"A better place," I said. "You know, Heaven."

Tina just looked at me. Otto didn't like the look.

Arianna spoke next. "It feels so creepy knowing someone did that—knowing they're out there somewhere."

"That they could be coming for us," Tina added.

I tried to calm their fears. "Could be just one of those things. Someone lost control. Doesn't mean they'll do it again."

Tina jumped up on her hands. She looked panicked, with abnormally wide-open eyes, a bloodless, pale face, and a half open mouth with her lips twitching. She took a few steps back, leaned against a wall, and grabbed a kitchen knife. "Get out, Otto."

I was shocked.

"What's wrong, Tina?" Arianna asked.

"It's him," she responded. "He did it."

"W—what? N—no." I couldn't believe she was doing this to me.

"Get out," she demanded.

"Tina—"

She cut me off. "Out!"

"Mary was my friend," I pleaded.

"Tina," Arianna said, but Tina cut her off.

She grew hysterical. "Out! Out! Out!" she screamed.

"You better leave," Arianna told me.

"But I..." I knew not what to say. Otto nodded and left. For a while, I stood alone outside in the rain.

I slowly went back to my trailer. Otto not know what got into Tina. She go nutty from stress maybe. I don't know. And oh poor Mary. When I got inside, I sat and thought of her. Oh, so sad. Later, there was a sudden knock. Oh, did this startle poor, sad Otto. I opened the door. It was the police.

"Excuse me, sir. Are you Otto Radowski?" he asked.

"Yessum."

"Can I come in and talk to you?"

Don't know why but I was nervous. "Um, yes," I answered. Let him in and agreed to talk. Had to. "Um, have a seat."

"Thank you," he said and took a seat in my plastic chair.

Otto sat on the bed. Policeman talked about what happened to Mary and offered condolences. I thanked him. What Otto really wanted was to not talk about this, but he continued.

He took out a notepad and pencil and ask how long I know Mary. I answer but he kept asking. Long time. It was long time. Why he need to know how long? How was I supposed to remember such things? His questions made me nervous and scatterbrained.

Next, he asked about our friendship. We were good friends, we were. There was a time when things happened, but it wasn't romantic, so I answered his question right when I told him "Just friends."

Oh, then he started asking me about the night. Not make old Otto happy, no, it did not. Not want to think about it but I did. I answered. Thinking about it all made me sad for Mary. Poor Mary, she such a good person. But he kept asking more questions, even though Otto sad. Then he stopped for a few seconds. Looked at Otto. Was he done?

No, he was not. Now he started asking Otto about Otto.

"How long have you been with this carnival?" policeman asked.

"Many years. I been here many years. Been doing show here many years."

"Can you tell me how many years?"

"I don't know how many. Long time."

"Can you guess how many?" he asked.

What did he want from me? Too much stress now, no time to math it up. "I don't know. Bill probably has records," says Otto.

"Is this your first carnival?"

"No. I been with many carnivals, since younger. Many years." Why did he need all this? So hard.

"How old were you when you took your first carnival job?"

"Years. I don't know. Don't want to think about that."

"I'm asking you to think about that," he said. He was serious. Otto best answer.

"In my twenties, I remember that." I tried to block out the years before but it came leaking back, though I fought it so.

"Were you always a Bozo the clown?"

"No, not until third outfit," then, after a recollection I said, "or four. It was three or four." I then remember. "Three. It was number three." I remember good, after thinking about it. "Oh so long ago. So many years."

"Have you enjoyed the carny life?"

"Yessum, much so. Had good times. Remember Doug and Pinhead Ollie, oh he funny. He one time caught pissing on Bill's doorstep. Bill not find funny so Ollie gone. Lots of people made Bill mad over years." I smiled thinking about it. "Some guy, can't remember his name or act too well, something like the Human Beef Patty Boy, or something, he had brain problems. Well, he got mad at Bill for something and tell him that if brains was needed to run a carnival Bill wouldn't be running no carnival. Oh, was Bill mad. Threw him out that night. Left him in some small West Virginia town. Wonder if he's dead. Not smart." I enjoyed telling old stories. It was good thinking about good times.

But then, as I paused, he broke in. "Mr. Radowski, why did you choose to become a carny?"

"Oh," I said as I tried to think. Hard to answer, but I had to say something or he would keep asking, so I answered. "Oh, what to say? There was stuff and there was other stuff, so it hard to say. Otto wanted to get away because of stuff but would I have chose this anyway? Would Otto have chosen this path without stuff happening? Otto don't know."

We sat quietly and he looked at me for maybe five seconds. "Otto, what are you hiding from me?"

I told him I tell everything he needs to know. Why he think I hide something? But what I tell him don't matter because he keep asking. Oh, didn't want to think about this, but I did. Oh, did I. Thoughts flood me, flood my old brain. I tell him things I don't want to think about. Things that were not important. But Otto answer. I talk and talk. So sad he ask me these things but he keep asking. Why was he doing this to me? I answered best I could but Otto didn't remember much and told him so. This was the truth. It was all fuzzy for Otto now, but policeman pushed on.

I left that town because things happened. Why these things happen to me? I was nice. Gave candy. Could that be it? Candy? Nice? I don't know. Otto just don't know. Had to leave, was accused, still don't know why but could see it in everybody's eyes. Oh, thinking back upset old Otto. Painful memories. But I kept talking, telling him until he stops Otto.

"Thank you. That's all I need to know."

"Mmhmm, good." I hoped he would leave, but he wouldn't yet. "I don't mean to be tough on you, Mr. Radowski," he said. "I just need to be thorough and learn everything I can about this past night and the victim's friends. You may not believe this, but I have a great deal of sympathy for you and everyone here. I used to live your life. I was a carny for a year and I still love carnivals."

"Oh, yeah?" I was breathing heavy. Otto catching breath and trying to understand what this all meant. Was he truthful? I had to say something, so I said, "It's a good life." And it was.

"Can I see your costume?"

"My costume?" Why he want to see that?

"Yes, your clown costume. I'm trying to picture

what you look like performing. You seem like you'd make a hell of a clown."

"Oh, okay." Was he joshing me? Really like Otto? I got up, still shaking from all the questions. Not feel right. Went to my closet and got out costume. Held it up to show him. "This is it."

He looked at it. "It's wet," he said

"Yessum, raining hard."

He looked at it again. "Thank you for your time." He stood up. "I am sorry for the loss of your friend. I will do my best to find the person responsible."

I just kind of nodded and mumbled, "Thank you."

Sweating from bad flashback. He leave and Otto just sit, shaking, for I don't know how long. Long.

Chapter 7

Tom Davis:

Bill took me to his trailer—the biggest on the back lot—which held his office and sleeping quarters. We sat in the office section with him taking a seat behind a small desk and me on the opposite side. As we sat, he held out a cigarette case. "Smoke?"

"Yes, please," I said, taking a cigarette. I couldn't help but notice the fancy silver cigarette case with the photo of a very attractive nude woman on it. "French case?"

"Good eye. I picked it up durin' the Great War."

"I fought in the second," I told him. Knowing the potential was there for us to quickly become sidetracked from the business at hand, I quickly moved on to the questioning. "Please tell me your full name."

"William John Harris."

"What were you doing between eleven o'clock until you discovered the body?"

He told me that he was in his trailer until Gino informed him that the victim had missed her show, and then he went to her trailer to find her and discovered the body.

"How long have you owned the carnival?" I asked.

"Oh, fourteen years."

"How did you start in the business?" I asked.

"After the war, I was werkin' as a cook. I hated it. Always hot back there, an' hated werkin' fer someone else. Was always havin' to take orders from a real asshole. I got enough o' that in the war. So I just started savin'. Always eatin' as cheaply as possible, never doin' anythin' er buyin' anythin'. Savin' every penny. When I started gittin' some money, I decided I wanted to run a carnival. I werked fer one before the war an' liked the travelin' to differen' towns an' entertainin' people, so I decided to take my savins an' put one together."

"That's lot of work."

"It was, but it was werth it. I had a dream, a vision fer what I wanted it to look an' be like. Modern rides an' fun with a classic look. Started off with a gay nineties theme, but has evolved into its own thing over the years, but always very visual. I like each exhibit an' ride to be its own little world, take the customers somewhere else. I'm very big into the visuals."

I liked his vision and wanted to hear more about it, but that's not why I was here. "How did you meet Mary?"

"She applied fer a job when I was puttin' together my first outfit. Hot girl, huge tits, so I hired her on the spot."

"She's been with you for a long time. How would you describe your relationship with her?"

"It's been great. I've been as close to her as anyone who has ever werked fer me. Those first few years were rough, payin' the bills an' jus' stayin' in business. She was someone I was able to talk to, a good listener. Always made me feel better." He wiped his eyes. "I'll miss her badly."

"Do you know of anyone who might have wanted her dead?" He paused, as if thinking. After a quiet moment I asked, "Can you think of anyone that might have done this?" Again, he paused. It seemed to me he was holding back. "I can't solve this if you don't tell me everything."

"Well, I don't want to make her soun' like a bad person er nothin', but it's like this. When a creepy guy was hittin' on her er touchin' her er whatever, well, she had her way o' gittin' back at guys like that. She had this collection o' keys. She'd always have one with her. She'd tell the guy it was a key to her room at some nearby motel, an' that he could have it fer a price. She only did this on the last night o' the carnival, an' always told the guys to meet her there the next night. I always told her this could go bad, but she just laughed it off. I think maybe one o' these creeps offed her."

His story was interesting, and the murder had occurred on the last night of the carnival. Maybe some guy decided to go to the motel early and found the key didn't work? This was worth checking into.

I turned my attention to the other carnies. I asked Bill for a record of all his employees.

"I got an account book right here," he told me as he opened his desk drawer. He pulled out a small notebook and handed it to me.

I asked him to tell me about the different carnies, their backgrounds, and their relationships with the victim. After we had covered everyone, I returned to the first carny Bill told me about, Gino Guglielmo, the man who wouldn't let me inside his trailer. He ran the kootch show. It seems that Gino wanted to fire Mary earlier that night because she hadn't shown up for her show. I realized that she had probably not shown up because she was already dead, but, as I had no other leads, I told Bill, "I'd like to speak to Mr. Guglielmo next."

I knocked on his door. He opened it and stuck his head out. "Yes?" he asked.

"Mr. Guglielmo, I'd like to ask you a few questions." He sighed and stepped out, shutting the door behind him. I tried to glance inside for the moment the door was open. I didn't notice anything suspicious. He lit up a cigar. Gino was a bald, slimy looking little fellow. Picture the guy you'd expect to be running the kootch show at a small-town carnival, and you'll picture Gino. He was crude, rude, and tactless.

"Mr. Guglielmo, how long have you known the victim?"

"Twelve years. Since I took over the girl show."

"How was your relationship with her?"

"Fine mostly. She could be flaky from time to time, and she drank too much—most strippers do. But when she was sober and working she was fine. She had the best tits in the show. I'm gonna miss her."

"I mean personally, did you get along with her?"

"Sure. She made me mad with the flaky shit sometimes, but most the girls have problems. I'm a forgiving guy, so it's just something I have to deal with. I got along with her fine most the time."

"When did you last see the victim?"

"Earlier tonight when she performed."

"And you didn't see her after that?"

"No, I was at the show all night."

"I understand she missed her last show?"

"Fuck yeah. I was pissed too. Thought I was going to have to fire the bitch. To miss the last show of the year told me she didn't care. But I guess she was probably dead, so looking back it probably was not her fault."

"What were you doing from eleven o'clock until Bill Harris found the body?"

"I was running things at the show."

"Did you leave the show tent at any time between eleven and when you went to see Harris?"

"No."

"Do you know of anyone who might have wanted to kill her?"

"It's probably some guy who saw her in the show, liked her rack, then she wouldn't put out for him. Or maybe she threatened to cry rape against some guy again. I don't know."

"What do you mean 'threatened to cry rape again'?"

"'Few years back, she accused some guy of rape but there was nothing to it."

"How do you know there was nothing to it?"

"There was no knife, no gun, nothing like that. She claimed the guy just forced himself in as she tried to push him off."

"So?"

"It's hard enough to get it in some dry hole without some broad struggling. As Thomas Paine said, 'You can't thread a moving needle.'"

I was sure Paine had not said that but it wasn't important so I let him continue.

"He probably ticked her off or offended her in some other way, so she claimed rape. I don't know. I like Mary so I didn't question it."

I was eager to turn the conversation back to a relevant topic. "What do you know about her selling fake motel room keys to overeager customers?"

"You heard about that?"

I nodded.

"She's been doing that for years," he told me.

"Do you know if she sold any keys tonight?"

"No. I don't know. I got a lot to deal with."

"Thank you for your time, Mr. Guglielmo."

I interviewed Popeye, whose real name was Gary, next. They called him Popeye because he could make his eyeballs pop out of his head. I had seen this kind of thing before, but it still made me uneasy seeing those two round eyeballs completely out of their sockets. He laughed at my reaction.

Gary was in his trailer when he heard Bill scream, "There's been a murder." He said he hadn't seen anything strange that night. He said he liked Mary. He did admit to being intimate with her a few years back, but said it was no big deal. They remained friendly, but not close.

When I knocked on the next door, I heard a yell inside. I was prepared to break it down when a female voice asked, "Who is it?"

"Police," I responded.

"Just a moment." A pretty young woman opened the door.

"May I come in? I'd like to ask you some questions."

"Yes, please."

I entered. There was another girl inside, a stunning blonde with no legs who was wearing a pajama top and shorts.

I told them I would like to speak to each of them alone. I hated to send either of them out into the mud and rain, but I didn't want them to influence each other's memories. I had no choice.

"Is that necessary?" the girl who had let me in asked. "My friend, she shouldn't be alone right now."

"I'm afraid it is," I said sympathetically. "I promise to make it quick."

"Well—"

"It's fine," the legless one broke in. "I'll step outside."

"Thank you," I said. She threw on a coat and, on her hands, walked out. "May I have a seat?" I asked the other girl.

"Sure, yes," she said and I grabbed a chair.

"I didn't get a chance to introduce myself earlier when I checked the trailers. I'm Police Chief Davis."

"I'm Arianna Lewis."

"I don't want to leave your friend out in the rain for too long, so I'll get right to it. Do you know of any enemies the victim may have had, or anyone that might have wanted her dead?"

"Well," she said with some hesitation, "there's this one thing she did. When—" she said then just stopped.

I knew it was an emotional time for everyone around her, so I didn't say anything. I waited for her to continue, which she soon did.

"When some guy was being too touchy, or persistent

in asking for some alone time with her, she would sell them bogus hotel room keys and tell them to meet her at some nearby motel the next night," she told me. "She said she had done it for years. She always took note of some motel near every town we were in so she could have a name and location ready. Only did it on the last night so they couldn't come back the next night and find her. I think she may have even asked an occasional guy to come back to the show the last night so she could pull the con on him then. I told her this was a bad idea, we all did."

"Did she sell any keys tonight?"

"Not that I know of, but I didn't watch any of her shows. She could have."

"Do you know if she asked any guys back tonight with the intention of selling keys?"

"None that I know of."

"Do you know of anyone associated with the carnival that might want her dead or have any motive to kill her?"

"No," she stated after a short pause.

"When was the last time you saw the victim?"

"Earlier in the night in the show tent."

"Before or after your last show?"

"Before. It was right after my second to last show— she went on after me."

"Did you notice anything suspicious during the evening?"

"Nothing out of the ordinary. I heard Gino screaming about something when I left—I didn't hear what it was. It was when I was leaving."

"When was that?"

"It was the end of my work night. I'm not sure of the time. It was shortly before Bill found Mary."

"Did you see anything after you left?"

"Nothing until Bill screamed, 'There's been a murder.'"

"Thank you for your time."

"Glad to help."

She stepped outside and the other girl came in. She was nervous, scared, and upset. Her eyes were red from crying and she was shaking. She lit a cigarette and we began to talk.

"I'm Chief Davis." She was silent. "Bill told me you're Tina Mortenson. Do I have that correct?"

"Yes," she responded sheepishly.

I decided to ease into things with her because of her apparent fragile mental state. "How long have you been with the carnival?"

"This is my second year."

"Like it?"

"Yes and no."

"What do you like about it?"

"The people I work with."

"And you don't like?"

"The job. The creepy men leering at me. But what's

a girl like me supposed to do. It's good money."

"Where were you between eleven o'clock and the discovery of the victim?"

"I finished my last show at eleven and went to my trailer to sleep shortly after."

"You were sleeping when you heard about the murder?"

"In bed, trying to fall asleep."

"When was the last time you saw the victim?"

"Backstage earlier this evening. Didn't speak with her."

"How much earlier?"

"Oh I don't know, maybe seven o'clock."

"This past night, did you see anything suspicious leading up to the crime?" I thought it best not to use the word murder around her.

"No, nothing," she answered. "It was a normal night until I heard Bill scream."

"Do you know of anyone who might have done this?"

"Otto," she said.

"Otto?" I asked.

"The Bozo clown. I don't know why, but it was him. He did it." She talked slowly and seriously as she told me this.

"How do you know he did it?" I asked.

She looked me in the eyes. "I was scared to be alone. Arianna, Otto, and I came back here after we heard the news, you know, to keep each other company." She put out her cigarette. "We were talking about Mary, about how kind she was. I suddenly thought about her cat, Roscoe. She loved that cat more than anything. Then Otto said he had the cat. I asked him why. He said Mary asked him to watch him. He couldn't say why. Well, this struck me as very strange. She loved that cat. She lived in a small trailer and wasn't going anywhere. Why would she give Otto Roscoe, even for a short time?"

I took notes as she spoke.

"Well, then Otto said that Mary was in a better place now," Tina continued. "That may not sound like much, but it was the *way* he said it, and the look in his eyes. He did it. He felt guilty and he was trying to comfort himself. He began to talk about how the killer may have lost control. How it may have been a mistake." She became emotional as she told me this last part.

"Have you told this to anyone?" I asked.

Tina took a deep breath and slowed down. "I talked about it with Arianna. She doesn't believe it. Arianna's a nice girl, but she's too trusting, too naive."

"Do you know of any past relationship or troubles between Otto and Mary?"

"None. I haven't witnessed much interaction between the two, but Otto seemed to like her very much."

"How could you tell?"

"Just the way he—" She paused for a second. "—the way he looked at her. The way he acted around her. It was like a disturbing sort of flirting."

"Have you observed any strange behavior from Otto?"

"Strange? Otto is nothing but strange. Sometimes the guy never says a word, but when he gets going, he rambles on and on, but no one ever knows what he is talking about. It's only when he is performing that he's coherent. He never talks about his past. Ask around, no one knows anything about the guy."

"Did you observe any other suspicious behavior from Otto before or after the murder?"

"I didn't see him before, and nothing else afterward except what I already told you. When I knew it was him, I made him leave."

"I see." I thanked Tina for her time and asked her where Otto's trailer was. She hadn't given me any real evidence, but he was the first person anyone had mentioned as a suspect, so I decided to speak with him next.

I walked to his trailer and knocked on the door. A man opened the door and I asked, "Excuse me, sir. Are you Otto Radowski?"

"Yessum," he said.

I asked him if I could come in and talk. He let me in.

I sat down in Radowski's trailer and began my interview with him. "Mr. Radowski, I suppose you know what happened tonight."

"Yes sir," he responded. "Mary dead. Very sad."

"Was she a friend of yours?" I asked.

"Yes. Very good friend. This hurts."

"I'm sorry to hear that. Please accept my condolences."

"Thank you."

I took out my notebook. "Mr. Radowski, how long have you known the victim?"

"I know her many years."

"How many?"

"Many. Yes, many years."

"You can't tell me how many?"

"Long time. She been here a long time. I been here longer. So I know her as long as she been here. Don't know how long that is. Bill probably has records."

"How well did you know her?"

"Good friend. We good friends."

"Were you romantically involved?"

"Oh no. Just friends."

"When did you last see her?"

"Two hours ago, or more. What time is it now? I seen her just after rain started."

"So tonight, shortly before her death?"

"Yessum."

"Where did you see her?"

"Backyard. Both going home for night."

"Did you have any conversation with her?"

"Yes," he said, but didn't expand on the conversation at all, just sat quietly after answering.

"Can you tell me what was said?" I asked.

"Yeah, uh, she said, 'Hey Otto.' I said, 'Hi,' I think.

Um, don't think she said anything before she asked, 'Can you watch my cat for a while?' I says, 'Yes.' Then we may have talked a little as we went to get her cat. Hmm. Poor Mary, she such a good person."

"Mr. Radowski, did the two of you have any other conversation?"

"No, I don't think so. Thought we might but as I think about it no. She may have said, 'I'll be right back,' when she went inside to get Roscoe, and 'thank you,' when she gave him to me. I said, 'my pleasure' and she closed her door."

"Why did she ask you to watch her cat?" I asked. This seemed like a strange request for her, or a bad lie from him.

"Dunno," he said. "Just asked me."

"She didn't give any reason?"

"No."

"Has she ever asked you to watch the cat before?"

"No, never."

"Was she acting any different than normal when you saw her?"

"She asked me to watch Roscoe. That was different. Otto like pussies just fine, but never have one of my own. Lots of work. A bit allergic, get sniffles, you know. But I guess I'll take care of poor Roscoe now."

"Mr. Radowski, was there anything else different about her?"

"Well, she seemed like she was in a bit of a hurry. Closed door quick after giving up Roscoe."

I paused to collect my thoughts, then moved on to asking about him. The problem was that he had a difficult time answering my questions. Sometimes, he would begin answering then begin to talk about something completely different. Other times I didn't know what he was talking about, and his over the top Charlie Chaplin like hand gestures were distracting. Was this a game he was playing with me, or was he always like this? Whatever the reason, he was a difficult interview.

When I asked about his past, it was especially frustrating. I had the feeling that there was something he didn't want me to know. He said he had been a carny since he was in his twenties, but when I asked why he chose the carny life, he would ramble incoherently. Finally I said, "Otto, what are you hiding from me?"

"Me? Hiding? Nothing. I tell everything."

"Then tell me, why did you go to work for a carnival?"

"I told you, sir, I wanted to get away, get away from it all. And carnival came calling. It was like destiny."

"Otto, what did you want to get away from?"

"My hometown. I wanted to get away from my friends, oh, yes, I did. And I did. Here I am." Otto smiled.

"Why did you want to get away from your friends?"

"They think I bad, think I done something bad, but I didn't, oh no. But they thinks I did, so they look at Otto differently. So I left."

"Otto, what did they think you did?"

"Be mean to little boy. I didn't do nothing, but they think I did, yessum."

"What do you mean, they thought you were mean to him?"

"They think I make him do things he not want to."

"What kind of things, Mr. Radowski?"

"Oh I try to forget all this. Bad things. Bad things."

"What bad things?"

"They think I touch him in special place."

"Did you?"

"No, no, I told you, I done nothing."

"Were you arrested?"

"No, no. No evidence, but people thought. And you know, you can't change that—no, no. Once people think it, they think it. It was fact to them, my hometown. Make me sad. So I leave."

"Why did they think you did it?"

"I don't know, don't remember now."

"There must have been a reason, Otto. Tell me the reason."

"I don't know. Because I nice to kid, maybe. Gave candy, time to time. Nothing more. But they think I did it. I not know why. Oh, oh, if only, but I not know. No thinks—what they think—not know."

When I first began to talk to him, he was more in control of himself. But, by this point, he had sped up his speech and his English became almost incomprehensible.

I decided to back off. Otto was the first viable suspect, and he just let on that he had been suspected in a sex crime once before. He also seemed nervous. If he had done it, I suspected it was a crime of passion, which meant there was a good chance he made a mistake, left some clue, which would link him to the crime. It was best not to let him know he was a suspect. He might slip up. More importantly, he was less likely to destroy any evidence before I got a warrant to search his trailer. He, like everyone, except Guglielmo, let me look around his trailer earlier, but that was a quick search. I was sure he wouldn't let me tear it apart without a warrant. But I would hold off on obtaining one for now in the hope that he slipped up. Radowski seemed genuinely broken up by what had happened, further adding to my belief that, if it was him, it was a spontaneous crime of passion. This would go along with the fact that the victim was killed with her own knife, and the no prints could be explained if he was still in costume and had gloves on. This led me to picturing him—as the clown—killing her. I decided to casually bring up his costume and ask to see it.

I acted as if the official interview was over. "Thank you. That's all I need to know."

"Mmhmm, good," he said, still appearing very anxious.

"I don't mean to be tough on you, Mr. Radowski. I just need to be thorough and learn everything I can about this past night and the victim's friends. You may not believe this, but I have a great deal of sympathy for you and everyone here. I used to live your life. I was a carny for a year and I still love carnivals."

"Oh, yeah? It's good life."

"Can I see your costume?"

"My costume?"

"Yes, your clown costume. I'm trying to picture what you look like performing. You seem like you'd make a hell of a clown."

He appeared to believe what I was saying.

Without hesitation, he jumped up. "Oh, okay." The interview had obviously shaken Otto, and he uneasily went to his closet and pulled out the costume. He held it out to show me. "This it."

It appeared clean and bloodless. It was wet.

"It's wet," I told him.

"Yessum, raining hard."

That was true.

"Thank you for your time," I said as I stood. "I am sorry for the loss of your friend. I will do my best to find the person responsible."

"Thank you."

After him, I decided I needed to speed up my interviews. I wanted to talk to as many persons as possible tonight to gauge their reactions and get fresh recollections, so I made my way from trailer to trailer, speaking with twenty-two carnies in quick succession. It turned out to be frustrating because I didn't get too much helpful information, but I did come away with a few items of interest. I learned that Radowski's strange speech and behavior wasn't some game he was playing with me—it was just how he was. Amy, a colored stripper, testified to how angry Gino was with the victim that night, as angry as she'd ever seen him, and it was her opinion that he "might" be guilty. She said that he was gone for a while when he went to look for her. She also told me about the hotel key scam. Shawn Keyhoe, who ran the "World of the Future" exhibit, saw Otto with the victim just after he closed up for the night, but he just saw them in passing and didn't have anything else to tell. A few persons spoke of a possible past sexual relationship between the victim and Bill. I made a note to ask Bill about that later. Some of the carnies already thought they had the case solved. The legless stripper thought it was Otto, three were certain it was Bill, another three thought it was Gino, and one moron was convinced aliens were responsible.

None had anything real to back up their assumptions with. It was clear I had my work cut out for me.

Chapter 8

Brian Stockton,
Sunday, November 1, 1953:

I was in my black '48 Chevrolet Fleetline early the next morning, smoking a cigarette and driving back to the fairgrounds. There had been a murder and the paper sent me to get the story. Finally, I had something real to write about, a real story.

The rain that fell hard all night had finally let up, but it was still a dreary morning. I arrived at the fairgrounds and parked in the muddy lot. A police car was the only other automobile there. I could feel a cold nip in the air as I exited my vehicle and discarded my cigarette butt.

As soon as I entered the midway, I saw Police Chief Davis coming toward the parking lot. We both stopped as we reached each other. Davis was your typical tough-guy cop. He wasn't big in stature, but you knew he wasn't to be messed with. He was a by-the-book type. He had fought in the war, but his hair had grown since then so he didn't have that military look. He liked me. We had a playful relationship.

"Brian," he said to me. "I didn't expect to see you here so early. Shouldn't you be passing out about now from a long night of drinking?"

"You know work comes first," I responded as I lit a cigarette. After some silence I asked, "So, what's the story here?"

"A girl was murdered," Tom informed me. "Grizzly. I have never seen anything like it."

"Any leads?" I asked.

"No smoking gun. Off the record, I suspect it was someone who works for the carnival."

"And they just happened to do it in your jurisdiction. Lucky you."

"Yeah, I know. Nothing I can do about that."

"Someone from county coming to handle it?"

"Looks like I'm handling the bulk of it. Listen, I have to get going."

"Can I get an official statement?"

"No comment at this time."

"Thank you. Good luck."

He nodded and marched off. An unsolved murder at a carnival. It was not the kind of thing I was used to covering. It would be a good challenge and I hoped it would help get me out of this small-town, get me to the bright lights and important stories. I walked through the mud to the carnies' living quarters.

The question was where to begin. I didn't want to start knocking on doors and wake anyone who might be sleeping, even though it was doubtful anyone was asleep after what had happened. I chose to wait for them to come out. I finished my cigarette and smoked another while I waited for someone to emerge from their trailer. I was on my third cigarette of the morning when I saw the first sign of life. The bearded lady came out of her trailer to have a smoke. What a sight she was in her pink robe and pink bunny slippers with that thick brown beard that you would expect to see on a lumberjack.

"Excuse me, miss," I called out as I walked over to her.

"What do you want?" she shot back, cold as ice.

"I'm with the local newspaper," I said.

"You're here to turn a tragedy into a story? I want no part of that," she snipped as she flicked her cigarette at me and went back into her trailer.

What a waste of a perfectly fine cigarette. I looked down at it, all that fine tobacco needlessly wasted. What a shame. Then I heard a noise behind me. It was time to put the cigarette out of my mind and get back to work. I saw two women emerge from a trailer. They looked worn out. One was the legless stripper I had seen hours earlier, and the other was that cute brunette who followed her on stage.

"Excuse me, excuse me," I called out as I ran over.

"What the hell do you want?" the legless one snapped.

"I'm a reporter with the local paper," I tried to explain.

She called me a jackal and "walked" away.

"I'm sorry," said her cute friend. "She's taking this really hard. We all are."

"I'm sorry. I'm not trying to cause any more pain, but if there's someone dangerous on the loose, the locals ought to know about it."

"I understand, and I know you're just doing your job," she said sympathetically. "If you come back in an hour I'll tell you whatever you want to know."

"That's very nice of you. I'll take you up on that." I held out my hand, "I'm Brian."

She smiled the cutest smile and said her name was Arianna. She looked worried and tired, but underneath it all, she looked like an angel. I looked forward to seeing her again.

I followed that encounter with a couple of nonproductive interviews. First, I saw a large, dirty looking man walking and ran up to him. "Excuse me, sir."

"Ya?" he responded.

"I'm Brian, a reporter with the local paper. I'd like to speak with you about what happened, if you can spare a moment."

"Aw, Jesus shit. All right, but make it quick, I ain't

slept all night an' gotta piss like a fuckin' mongoose." That bizarre expression was the beginning of a conversation that I am sure killed some of my brain cells.

"I'll be quick. What do you know about what happened here?"

"A stripper was murdered last night. Bloody mess."

"Bloody mess? You saw the crime scene?"

"I foun' her. Wish I hadn'. Who knows what paralogical mess that caused in my head? I won' ever fergit it, that's fer sure."

"How did you come to find her?"

"She missed her show, an' I wen' to git her. Figured she was drunk. When she didn' answer, I let myself in."

"What did you see?"

"Mary on the bed, face down in a pool o' blood. Nothin' else—I got right out."

"Any idea who might have done this?"

"How would I know? Could be some guy who saw her show, thought he was some real Don John an' started makin' his moves on her an' got rejected. Er some local transent who stumbled into the fairgrounds. Anyone is possible. I ain't a fuckin' cop detective."

I knew it was time to wrap this up, if for no other reason than I did not want to waste more of my life talking to this guy. I made that decision as soon as he said "transent" instead of "transient." I decided to find out who I was interviewing then end it.

"What do you do here?" I asked.

"I own the place—I mean the carnival, not the fairgrounds."

"Uh, I see," I said as I tried to grasp what he just told me.

This man didn't seem smart enough to work at a carnival, much less own one. I couldn't figure out how a man like this could even get together the money to own a carnival. From what I could tell, he was an idiot. I could have spent a long time questioning him to find out how this happened, but, on top of being near brain dead, he was so dirty and disgusting that I just wanted to get away from him. I asked my final question: "And your name is?"

"Bill Harris."

"Thank you. That's all I need."

"Good," he grunted and walked off.

At this time more people started coming outside so I did a few short interviews, one with the sword swallower, one with the cyclops—the cave in his forehead was real, the eye from the act wasn't—and one with the guy that ran the strength testing booth. None of those I interviewed knew much, just that a stripper named Mary, whose stage name was Busty Laroche, had been killed. She was, by all accounts, a sweet woman. Everyone I talked to was still in shock.

Then someone tapped me on the shoulder. It was the attractive Arianna. "Hi," she said.

"Oh, hey, good to see you."

"I can talk now if you want to."

"Yeah, sure, um, can you tell me—"

"Would you like some coffee?" she interrupted. "I have some in my trailer."

"Sure, thanks."

Truth is I didn't care for coffee, but I liked being around Arianna and was happy for an excuse to be alone with her, even if it was a horrible idea on her part to invite a stranger back to her trailer the night after one of her own had been murdered.

"This way," she said.

While following her, I looked at her nice figure and long brown hair. It was nice to watch her.

The inside of Arianna's small trailer was nicer than I expected. It was cozy. She did a good job of making it feel like a real home. She made the coffee then we sat down. "What would you like to know?" she asked politely.

I knew jumping right into the murder would be hard on her, and, honestly, I needed more information than that. So I began with, "Can you tell me a little about yourself?"

She smiled, looked down, and picked at a fingernail. Then she glanced back up. "Like what?" she asked.

"Where are you from?"

"I was raised in Kansas. I'm just a small-town girl, trying to make it in the world."

"How long have you been with this outfit?"

"A year and a half."

"How'd you hook-up with the carnival?"

"They came through my town. It was spring. I was working as a waitress in a little diner on Route 66. I saw all of these people passing through, passing from one end of the country to the other. I wanted that. I wanted to see the world. When the carnival came to town, I heard they were looking for showgirls. Well, I decided I could take my clothes off if it meant seeing the United States. Bill and Gino had me meet them in Bill's trailer and hired me on the spot."

I wondered if anything happened at that meeting but did not ask. "And the stripping doesn't bother you?"

"Oh, it did at first. I was a good girl—" She smiled. "—a small-town virgin. But I told myself, 'it's just the human body. It's natural and beautiful.' In my mind, I was already rebelling from my Catholic upbringing. I had spent enough time following the rules of a religion that I did not believe in and worshipping a God that does not exist, and even if he does, he certainly doesn't care if I take my clothes off. After all, he's supposedly the one who created my body, right?"

"Right," I nodded as I thought about what a terrific job he did creating her.

"Well, that was it. My chance to see the country had come and no phony religion or fictional God was going to stop me."

"So, how has it worked out? Have you enjoyed your travels?"

"I have." She smiled, paused, and then sighed. "Until last night."

Since she brought it up, I dove into the serious questions. "Can you tell me what happened?"

"Well, we had just closed. I had taken a slow walk in the rain after the show before returning to my trailer. I got back and was just sitting around thinking when I heard the scream, 'There's been a murder!'" She took a deep breath. "It was Mary. I heard that someone stabbed her in the neck. That's all I know." She paused again. "She was so caring and nice. Never did anybody no harm. And she loved her cat Roscoe so." Arianna began crying. "Who could do such a terrible thing?"

She broke down. I didn't know what to say to console her. What could I say? Nothing would bring her friend back. I just patted her shoulder and sat quietly.

After a few moments, she composed herself. "I'm so sorry."

"Don't be. Do you want to be alone?"

"No, talking helps. Please stay. We can continue the interview."

"Very well," I said and proceeded to ask her about her fellow carnies.

She was a sweet girl and didn't say a bad word about anyone, even when I suspected that she wanted to.

She told me about Bill, the carnival's owner. She

said he was a good owner and ran a tight ship. I knew there was something not right about that slob, but she didn't say a negative word about him.

She talked about Tina, the legless girl who'd wanted nothing to do with me earlier. Arianna said that Tina was usually much nicer, but that this event really shook her up. She told me about a confrontation Tina had with Otto over the past night. Otto Radowski was the Bozo the Clown that had harassed me. Arianna said Radowski was "a sweet old man" but added that he was "a little odd." No one knew much about his past. He was a quiet man who didn't talk much and, when he did, people weren't always sure what he was talking about. Arianna laughed as she told me this. It was good seeing her smile. She wiped the tears away from her eyes. I could see that talking about her fellow carnies helped her cope. Anyway, she returned to the incident with Otto and Tina. Apparently, Otto had said some things that convinced Tina that he was the killer.

"What exactly did he say?" I asked Arianna.

"She's in a better place now, stuff like that."

"I see." This didn't seem incriminating.

"Oh, and that he had her cat."

"He had the victim's cat?" I asked. Now this was important.

"He said Mary asked him to watch Roscoe."

"Did he say why?"

"No, he didn't say anything else about it."

"That's strange." I knew I'd have to question the clown about this. I saw a look of worry return to Arianna's face so, for her sake, I asked her about others to take her mind off the tragedy.

I spent close to an hour interviewing her and learning about her coworkers. She seemed to be holding together okay when I left. I felt good about getting to know and comfort her and was happy I accomplished some good work as well. I now knew a lot more about the people she worked with.

Next, I spoke briefly to Serpent Boy, whose given name was Jerry. I could see from meeting him that the scales he had worn during the show were fake, but the lack of hands and feet was real. Like most of the carnies, he didn't give me any new information. When I asked him about Otto Radowski, he repeated what others had said. "He's a nice guy. He's a nut." He, just like everyone else, did not know much about the clown's past.

Before writing up the story, I wanted to speak to Radowski. He sounded like an interesting fellow, and he had been watching the victim's cat last night, so I thought he might know something. Unfortunately, Otto wasn't in a talkative mood. When I knocked, he answered the door immediately.

"What do you want?" he demanded.

"I'm with the local paper—"

Before I could get out anything else, he shook his head. "Otto no talk now," he exclaimed.

Then he slammed the door in my face. Inside his trailer, he followed that with a scream that was both horrible and pathetic.

Now might not be the best time to speak with him, I thought.

I made my way back to my office to write up the story…well, to write up what I had so far. I knew there would be changes throughout the day, depending on what I learned, and what new developments might occur. I was excited to write it up. I felt like a real reporter, not a small-town hack.

Chapter 9

Arianna Lewis:

I had spent the night with Tina. We talked and consoled each other while the rain fell outside. By morning, the rain had stopped. We sat together in her trailer, not talking much, just being there for each other. We were both still shaken from what had occurred. I hurt so bad inside. I felt I was holding myself together fairly well, considering. Tina, on the other hand, was a wreck. She had been shaking all night long, and she was convinced that the murderer had been in this trailer with us hours earlier.

I attempted to ease her concerns about Otto, but it did no good. She was certain he was guilty based on his behavior after the murder. I didn't put much stock into it. We all were in shock and everyone had his or her own way of dealing with this type of tragedy. I knew Otto liked Mary and chalked up his behavior to grief, but Tina felt differently.

I must say that the possibility that the murderer was one of us carnies very much upset me. It was a combination of fear and of just knowing that someone I had been friendly—or friends—with, could do that. It was a nauseating feeling.

Finally, I couldn't take being in this small room any longer. It was morning and I heard voices outside. "Tina," I said, "why don't we step outside for some air?"

"I don't want to see people," she said shakily. "And what if *he's* out there?"

"We can't stay locked up in here forever. It'll be good for both of us to get out."

"I don't know."

"Everyone is going through the same pain we are, and if you don't want to talk they won't push you."

She was silent for a moment. "All right," she finally agreed. "For a little bit?" She raised her voice and eyebrows, as if that was a question.

"We'll come back if you get uncomfortable," I assured her.

She did not respond and we were quiet while I put on my shoes.

As soon as we stepped out the door, a man came running over. Couldn't he see that we were upset? Tina didn't take kindly to him.

"Jackal," Tina exclaimed, after he told us he was a reporter with the local paper, and left as quickly as she could.

His coming over was inconsiderate, but he was only doing his job and he wasn't trying to hurt us, so I tried to be understanding.

"I'm sorry. She's taking this really hard. We all are," I explained.

"I'm sorry," he said and seemed sincere. "I'm not trying to cause any more pain, but if there's someone dangerous on the loose, the locals ought to know about it."

"I understand, and I know you're just doing your job. If you come back in an hour, I'll tell you whatever you want to know."

"That's very nice of you. I'll take you up on that." He smiled. "I'm Brian," he told me as he extended his hand.

"Arianna," I said.

He nodded and left. Brian had dark hair, was perhaps an inch under six feet tall, was slim, and appeared fit. He had high cheekbones but there was also something rugged about his face.

He was cute and seemed nice. I was glad that I would see him again.

Later that day I saw Gino and headed his way.

"Lewis, how are you holding up, doll?" he asked me as I approached him.

"Could be better, obviously. I feel so sad for Mary,

and I'm scared because the person who did this is still out there. I can't wait to leave this town."

"Don't you mean you can't wait to leave this carnival? You know the killa is among us, right?"

That was a dreadful thought. "Oh, I hope not. I can't even imagine that."

"You better come to grips with it. It's the most logical explanation."

I hated hearing this and found the idea difficult to accept. These people had been like family to me. While I had a hard time accepting it emotionally, logically I knew it was probably true. One of my friends with the carnival was likely the killer.

Gino clearly had an easier time coming to grips with the possibility. "I've been watching everybody," he told me, "looking for a sign, some clue as to who the guilty party is."

"What if it's a local townsperson?" I asked.

"No," he shook his head. "It's someone here. I know it is. The smell of evil is in the air." His eyes grew wide as he said this and, for the first time, I noticed his resemblance to Peter Lorre—a squatty, greasy Peter Lorre. "Be careful," he warned me. "The killa could strike again at any moment."

The thought sent chills down my spine. Needless to say, talking to Gino did not make me feel any better.

Then I spotted that reporter standing alone, writing something down. I walked over and tapped him on the shoulder.

He turned and I said, "Hi."

He kind of stumbled with his words for a moment until he finally got out, "Oh, hey. Good to see you."

It was cute.

"I can talk now if you want to," I told him.

"Yeah, sure, um…" He took out a notepad. "Can you tell me—"

I cut him off because I was sick of standing around. "Would you like some coffee?" I asked. "I have some in my trailer."

"Sure, thanks," he said, which was good because it gave me an excuse to bring him somewhere where we could sit down.

"This way," I said and started walking. We were both silent on the walk there and while I made the coffee. When it was finished, I sat across from him. "What would you like to know?"

He surprised me by asking me to tell him a little about myself. I expected we were only here to talk about the murder. Was he flirting with me? It seemed like an inappropriate time for such a thing, but he was cute and a nice distraction, so I asked him, "Like what?"

We talked about my start with the carnival. When we got to what I actually do, he asked whether it bothered me. That's what everyone wants to know. They think it must bother me or that something is wrong with me—I'll admit that many of the girls I work with do have issues. Stripping did bother me at first, but I saw this as a good opportunity, and I knew it was just the human body, so I convinced myself intellectually that there was nothing wrong with it, and eventually my embarrassment subsided. I was honest with him. After I explained this to him, he nodded and gave a bit of a smile. I think I might have been embarrassing him.

This light conversation did not last long. We soon turned to the murder. I told him what I knew and then talked about Mary. That's when I cried. Thoughts of her flooded into my head. As these thoughts overtook me, I had a complete collapse. It was inevitable, but I wish I wouldn't have made him sit through my crying, though it was nice having him around after I composed myself. I asked him to continue.

He moved on to asking me about the other carnies. I don't know if he was just trying to get a feel of what everyone was like, attempting to find some clue to the murder, or just making conversation, but to me it didn't matter. He was sweet, and it was good to talk. When he finally left, I was feeling better than before he arrived, and my head was clearer. I still wasn't happy, but I was under control.

Chapter 10

Bill Harris:

I sat down at my desk an' put my feet up. We were stuck here indefinitely, Goddamn it! I wanted to go home. We all wanted to fuckin' go home. My empty house in Florida was waitin' fer me. It was the offseason an' time to git there. I don't like to complain' 'bout my health, but I been havin' back pains half the summer. I needed to relax. Damn copper keepin' us here.

Ah shit, if someone in this group killed one o' my attractions, I wanted to know 'bout it. They should be caught. We can't have this become a habit. At first, I thought it was an outsider. Some perv who came to see the strippers, propositioned her, an' when she said no, let her have it. Now I ain't so sure. That cop keeps askin' 'bout all my werkers, like he's convinced it's someone on my lot. A carny. But who? I thought on it some.

First, I think it might be Gary, who'd been with me fer years doin' his Popeye bit. Somethin' 'bout him ain't right. When I look in those eyes, those goddamn eyes. Then I thought 'bout someone else from the Freak Show: Theodore. Could he be the one? The guy don't do well with women an' is a bit strange. Aw shit, how could he do it? Boy ain't got no arms er legs.

Could it be a broad? That beautiful Negress Amy didn' git along well with her an' some others. Stuck up bitch. Er could those rumers be right? Shit almighty, could it be Otto? The guy always seemed so kind, 'spec when he's razzin' a mark. He is quiet, strange, a loner. *Shit, I don't fuckin' know.* I just hoped that flat foot would figure it out soon.

This was all goin' through my head when a knock came at the door. 'Cause o' this I was already in a bad mood when I answers it. It was a priest. "Yes?"

"Hello. I'm Father O'Leary of the—"

"What do you want?"

"First, let me offer my condolences for the terrible tragedy that has taken place. Times like this can be trying. That is why I am here, to offer comfort and support to any among you who desire it."

This was all we fuckin' needed. "Jesus Arnold Christ can't help us now. He should o' been here with his magic wine to stop the murder."

"The Lord works in mysterious way, my son. He is showing his love by testing you."

"I don't ga time fer your bullshit mumbo jumbo."

He wouldn' take a hint an' just kept on talkin'. "I sense you do not believe in our Lord. I can still help you. I am here to help all God's children, whether you've accepted our Lord or not."

At that, I screamed, "Git the fuck off the lot," an' slammed the door in his face.

What fuckin' religious domination has priests that act like that? I was sure the Lord would not approve o' his behavior. Why did he think I didn' accept the Lord just 'cause I didn' want his bullshit? Mr. Preacher didn' help my mood.

I made some coffee an' tried to relax, but the sadness o' the murder combined with my anger at Mr. Preacher, made that impossible. I decided I needed to git out o' the trailer.

As soon as I stepped out, some guy ran up to me. I know I seen this guy before but couldn' place who he was. He did have a streakin' resemblance to an old buddy o' mine, Fish-eye Fred Hastings, from Whynot, Missouri, 'spec this guy had feet instead o' flippers, so it wasn' Fish-eye. He was holdin' a pad o' paper. Then I thought I remembered who he was—that reporter I had spoken with a few hours earlier.

"Excuse me, sir," he says.

"What do you want?"

He extended his han' to shake. "I'd like to speak with you if I may."

Someone else wantin' somethin' from me. Well, he'd git my mind off Mr. Preacher. "Sure, why not? You're that reporter, right?"

"Yes, I am," he said.

I hit the head on the nail with that one. "What do you want to know?" I asked.

"First, I'd like to offer my sympathy over what happened."

I just grunted in response. What was I supposed to say to that? Then he asked me 'bout Mary, how long she been workin' for me, 'bout our relationship, stuff like that. He seemed to enjoy talkin' to me an' the conversation did help me git my mind off that preacher, but thinkin' o' Mary had brought me down again. I needed away from this guy. As he was writin' my last answer, I says, "Listen, I need to be done with this."

"I understand. Thank you for your time," he said an' walked off.

I went back inside jus' to be alone.

Chapter 11

Tom Davis:

I began the day by stopping at the only nearby motel, which was just on the outskirts of town. The owner told me he hadn't noticed anyone stop by. One couple was staying there, and those were the only persons he saw last night.

My next stop was to see Judge Taylor. I presented to him the little evidence I had against Gino Guglielmo. It wasn't much but I was hoping to get a warrant to search his trailer based on the fact that Guglielmo was angry with her earlier that night and left his show to check for her. Taylor realized the clock was ticking on this and issued the warrant. I took it to the fairgrounds.

As I entered the midway, I saw that reporter approach me. "Brian," I said, acknowledging him.

I had been up all night and had a long day ahead. I didn't need him asking me questions now. I tried to be as polite as I had time to be and answered a few of his questions before telling him I needed to get going. Unfortunately, I knew he'd soon be bothering me again.

I walked toward Bill's trailer and, when I saw Brian was no longer in sight, I changed direction, went to Guglielmo's, and knocked.

Guglielmo opened the door. "What do you want?" he snarled.

"I have a warrant to search your trailer," I said as I held it up.

"Aw, shit," he responded. "Just don't mess it up too bad."

After that, he was quiet.

As I entered, the first thing I noticed was that the inside of his trailer smelled like old cheese and cheap cigars. I don't know what Guglielmo did in here, but everything was greasy. It was as if someone spilled some kind of cooking oil over every single thing he had and just tried to wipe it off, leaving everything with a thin but noticeable coat. I looked around, opened drawers, picked up and looked under every item in there, went through all of his clothes, and checked out every inch of the tiny bathroom. The trailer was small so it did not take me long to look everywhere. I found nothing suspicious.

After I finished at Guglielmo's place, I went and knocked on Bill's door. I asked him to show me around the carnival. I checked every almost exhibit and stand, but unfortunately, because time was of the essence, I didn't have time to personally check some of the larger exhibits, such as the Funhouse—though I would have loved to—so I sent back other officers to check those later. Everyone was very cooperative. Unfortunately, I didn't find a thing.

When I returned to the station, the last thing I wanted to do was talk to that damn reporter, so of course he showed up minutes after me. I was able to get rid of him this time by explaining that even if I had a suspect, I wouldn't want it reported. I knew he'd be back, but this gave me some temporary relief from him.

Next, I assembled all of my men for a meeting. I had Paul bring them in early that morning to wait for me. We were a small department, nine men in total, but no detectives. We would have to make do. I opened by explaining the details of the case and ordered my men not to talk to anyone about it. I picked two men to go to the fairgrounds and look over the area, both the scene itself and surrounding grounds, and to pay special attention to the perimeter of the grounds, looking for anything suspicious, such as signs of someone leaving by some way other than the main entrance. I had done this before leaving after my interviews, but I wanted a second opinion, and for the area to be viewed in the daylight. I didn't expect them to find anything, but thought it would be good to have a fresh set of eyes check it out. I also told them to check all of the exhibits since I hadn't had time to search the larger ones. Then I put everyone under the charge of my deputy-chief. I explained that, since I was the only one with detective experience, I would take on this case personally and spend all of my time on it, leaving Inzalaco to run the day-to-day operations of the department. If there was anything unrelated to the murder that came up, I was not to be bothered with it. At that moment, we were interrupted by a phone call. It was Detective Perry so I took it. It was bad news. The only fingerprints on the knife were from the victim and hers was the only blood found. The coroner's report and the report from the lab, both of which he told me were on their way to me via courier, also offered no leads, no physical evidence. When I finished the call, I told my men to get to work.

Perry's call frustrated me, but I soon put it out of my mind and focused on the case. I sent another one of my men to the fairgrounds to bring back a few of the woman's friends—friends who had spent some time in her trailer. He returned with three strippers, one of whom was Tina Mortenson. Two of them said the victim owned a knife similar to the murder weapon, but could not say for sure if it was the same knife. There was another duplicate one still in a kitchen drawer in the trailer, so the knife was probably hers.

If it was hers, maybe the killing wasn't premeditated. Or maybe it was, but the murderer approached her with another weapon, or simply threatened her with his hands, then spotted the knife and decided to use it. I didn't know. The truth is I had nothing. All of this was simply supposition, nothing more. While I was looking over my interview notes, I received a return phone call from the sheriff in the town where Otto Radowski used to live. I had put in the call when I first returned from the fairgrounds and the sheriff there had promised to talk to some of the old-timers and look through the files then get back to me.

"So, what did you find out?" I asked.

"Otto Radowski was a former factory worker. He left town after he was accused of inappropriately touching a child."

"I see."

"It was one boy who made the allegation. He claimed that Radowski had grabbed and fondled him numerous times. As far as I'm concerned there is nothing to it. The boy who told it was known for making up stories to get attention. He still lives in the town and even now, these many years later, has the same reputation for lying. People were willing to believe the story because Radowski was considered odd, but the boy's story kept changing and, knowing what I know about Palek, the accuser, I am sure that Radowski is innocent."

"Interesting. Thanks for the information."

"Anything I can do to help. Let me know if you need anything else."

"Will do. It was good talking to you."

"Bye."

"Bye." I hung up. In spite of the sheriff's opinion, I decided to have another talk with Radowski.

I was walking to the door when the officers I had sent to look over the fairgrounds returned. "Find anything?" I asked.

"Not a thing," Donald answered. "It was unsettling going through that devil funhouse after a murder."

Terry, the other officer, nodded in agreement. "We didn't spend any more time in there than we needed to."

"Well, thanks for looking. I have to head down there to do another interview." I left them and drove over to see Radowski.

As I walked through the fairgrounds, I heard Brian call out "Chief, sir."

I couldn't escape that damned reporter. I had spoken with him twice already that day. He couldn't possibly expect that I'd tell him something new now. He must have hoped I would, because he came up and kept asking questions.

I shot him right down and told him that I'd haul him in if he didn't walk away. He obliged and I continued on my way.

I knocked on Radowski's door. He answered. I asked if I could come in.

"Yessum, certainly," he said and let me into his trailer. He was very polite. We began with some small talk.

After some casual conversation, I asked, "Mr. Radowski, what can you tell me about the allegation that you inappropriately touched a child before joining the carnival?"

His face turned white. He again denied the allegation. No matter how I phrased it or what I asked, he denied having any contact with the boy. As I watched him speak, I knew he was telling me the truth. Of course, I'd still investigate him. Just because he didn't fondle that boy doesn't mean he didn't commit this murder. I could not cross a suspect off the list because he didn't commit a different crime, but pursuing these past allegations, I felt, would not get me anywhere.

"Well, thank you for your time, Mr. Radowski."

He just nodded back.

I spoke to a few more carnies—a few I didn't speak to long enough during the first, rushed interviews—finishing with Betty Bates, whose act was something called "The Brainless Woman." Based on the conversation with her I concluded that act fit her perfectly. After I left her, some carnival worker I spoke to briefly last night approached me. He came up to me and offered to buy my soul. I didn't get the joke, so just said "no thanks," and kept walking.

On my way to my car, Gino Guglielmo came running up to me. "Stop, Chief." He got to me and stopped. "I forgot to tell you something when we talked."

"What is it?" I asked.

"You asked me about anyone that would want to kill Mary."

"Yes?"

"Well, I'm sure it ain't nothing, but our first night here she had a little tussle with a customer. Said he was getting fresh. I kicked him out and that was that."

This was the first I heard of this possibly important information. I took out my notepad. "Can you describe this man?"

"Yeah, yeah, I saw him good. He wasn't too tall or short. Bald I think, maybe had some hair, um, wearing a brown suit, might have had a moustache."

I wrote down this completely useless description then questioned him further in the hopes it might help him remember. "How old would you say this man was?"

"Olda I think. Sixtyish maybe."

"Sixtyish," I said under my breath as I wrote it down.

"But maybe not," he then added. "It was dark in there. He could have been thirty, for all I know."

"Thirty to sixty," I said as I wrote. "Hair color?"

"Bald," Guglielmo said confidently then, as I was writing this down, he said, "or maybe grey hair. Maybe both. I have a picture of both in my mind."

"How would you describe his build?"

"Skinner guy, I think. Maybe not. He was sitting down when I approached him, and I didn't look down and check out his body when he stood up, so it's hard to say. He wasn't fat."

"Any distinctive features?"

"No," he said and after a pause added, "none that I remember."

I had hoped that by questioning him further I could nail down some description, but it wasn't any use, since every time he said he thought he knew something, he followed by saying the complete opposite might be true. I closed my notebook. "Thank you. This will be helpful," I said and, despite his lack of description, I wasn't lying. If we could find someone else who witnessed this altercation and could confirm it happened, it would most definitely be a lead worth checking into.

I went and talked to the other girls in the show, but unfortunately learned that none of them witnessed the incident.

Chapter 12

Otto Radowski:

I no sleep none over the night. Too much happening, too depressed. Poor Mary. So sad. I hurt inside thinking of her. I hated the thought of never seeing her again. I wanted her back so bad—to undo what had been done. I cried a lot. Finally, after Otto had a really big cry I relax some, just sit back and remember good times. There was lots of them to remember.

I eat a little later. When I finally relax just a little bit, knock comes.

The policeman.

Suddenly I have bad feeling inside.

"Mr. Radowski, may I come in?" he asked.

"Yessum, certainly." I let him in. What else to do? He sat and I sat.

"How are you holding up?" he asked me.

It took me a few seconds to answer. What was the purpose of this question, I wondered. Was he really concerned? Finally, I said, "Best as I can be. Best as I can."

"Do you like it here? Like your job?"

I confused about why he asked, but answered, "Yes I do. Love my job. Love atmosphere. Love people here."

"Why did you become a carny again? I mean, what about the job itself attracted you?"

"Um…" I thought back. Why he asking all this again? "I liked carnivals and like the idea of making people happy so, when I wanted to get away, I came across a town where a carnival was and thought it was perfect. And it was."

"Mr. Radowski, what can you tell me about the allegation that you inappropriately touched a child before joining the carnival?"

My heart sank. "Oh, that," I said. "I already told you about that. I try to leave that behind, but it follows me. Otto didn't touch that kid."

"So why did he say you did?" he asks.

"Otto not know."

"You don't know why he accused you of touching him?"

"No. No idea."

"Did you have any past interactions with him?"

"No. He just another boy around the neighborhood. Otto not know him specifically."

"So you never touched him in any way when you were alone with him?"

"No, nothing." I wished he would stop asking. It so depressed me to think about it.

"So you are standing by the claim that you don't know why people think you did this?"

"Yes. They just said it. I don't know why. Wish I did." Oh I could see he didn't believe me. I wanted to cry.

"Well, thank you for your time, Mr. Radowski."

And that was it. He left. He didn't believe me. I knew it. Otto now a broken mess. Oh, the pain Otto felt. Oh, the pain.

Chapter 13

Brian Stockton:

Murder at the Fairgrounds" would be the headline in tomorrow's paper. My job now was to follow the case and learn all I could through my own investigation. I was excited about the opportunity to cover a story such as this. I needed to get right to work and see if I could uncover any leads that I could add to tomorrow's story. I went to the police station.

When I arrived at the station, the chief acted annoyed to see me, but I knew he was putting on a front.

"Not you," he said on seeing me. "What do you want?"

"You know why I'm here. What can you tell me about the murder?"

"Nothing. Go away."

"Nothing? Come on, do you have any suspects?"

"Too soon to say."

"We both know that if a murderer is caught, he is usually caught quickly. I know you have a suspect."

"Brian, listen." He looked me in the eyes. "Even if I had a suspect I wouldn't want it reported. He can't know he's a suspect."

I took out my notepad to write a note. "So you have one male suspect, got it." I spoke each word as I wrote.

"Brian, leave," he said sternly.

"All right, all right. But you know I'll keep coming back until I get something."

He shook his head and sighed. "I know."

My next stop was at a diner for lunch. I was starving. After that, I went to the fairgrounds. I lit a cigarette as I stepped out of my car and walked toward the fairgrounds. It was interesting seeing the entire carnival set up but with no people on site. I thought they'd be taking things down by now. I guess they knew they'd be here a while. Or perhaps the police chief asked them to leave everything as it was. Either way, it was a lonely midway.

It brought out thoughts of my lonely life. Thirty years old and still stuck with a rube paper. I wanted the exciting stories and large audience of a big city paper. I wanted the big city life. Well, I now had a real story to cover. I hoped it would put me on the map. A murder mystery like this was my opportunity.

I went from the midway to the backyard, which was

the carnies' living area. I saw the fat lady walking alone, so I approached her. "Excuse me. I'm a reporter for the local paper."

"And you want to ask me a few questions?"

"If I may."

"Sure, I don't mind. In fact, I can use the company."

"Okay. Where would you like to do this?" I asked.

"I was just going back to my trailer for lunch. Can we do it there?"

"Sure."

"Great," she said and began walking. "This way."

"By the way, I'm Brian," I said as we walked.

"It's nice to meet you, Brian. My name is Ingrid." She spoke very pleasantly, which was especially notable considering how some of the other carnies had been.

"It's nice to meet you too," I said.

We entered her home and sat down.

"Do you want anything to eat?"

"No, thank you." I was not looking forward to seeing what a seven-hundred pound woman ate. I was surprised to see her grab a plate of vegetables off her counter. There were celery and carrot sticks, broccoli and zucchini slices. I hated zucchini. What a vile vegetable. I didn't understand how anyone could eat that swill, but there it was on her plate. "If you don't mind me asking, how do you keep on all of that weight eating like that?"

"It only takes me a big meal here and there to keep the weight on. As I got older, I realized that I'd much rather eat like this. I'm not gaining weight anymore, but I'm not losing any, either. Maybe one day I'll give up the carny life and try to shed a few pounds."

"So you don't like being…" I paused as I searched for the right words. "…that size?"

"Not anymore. Not that I ever actually liked it, it was just that I didn't used to care one way or the other. But as I got older, and larger, the weight began to cause problems. I'm not really able to do much anymore. I can't even do simple things like shop for myself. It hurts to walk that much. My balance isn't very good, either. If I fall over, I am unable to get up on my own. It's not a great way to live, but on the plus side, I get paid to just sit and let people look at me."

I smiled. "So no plans on an immediate change of careers?"

"Oh no," she said. "I don't want to learn a new skill now that I have this one mastered."

We both laughed.

"What do you think about the people you work with?"

"On the whole, I like them very much. It's one of the things I like about my job."

"Yes, that's been a common answer around here. You seem like a close group."

"We are. That makes what happened so—" She choked up and stopped.

"I'm sorry, I didn't mean to—"

"No, it's okay," she said as she wiped tears from her eyes. "It's what we're here to talk about, isn't it?"

"Partly, yes," I acknowledged. "Well, now that we're on the subject, how well did you know the victim?"

"We weren't best friends or anything like that, but we got along great, spent many nights talking…well, about nothing really, just shooting the breeze." Tears formed in Ingrid's eyes. "I'm going to miss her so much. And the way she went. I can't even begin to imagine her fear." She stopped for a moment and cried.

Scenes like this always made me uncomfortable, but I had no choice except to wait it out. It wasn't long before she wiped her eyes and regained her composure.

"I just have to keep reminding myself that she's in a better place now."

"Do you suspect anyone?"

At my question, she turned pale. "Bill," she said in a whisper.

"Bill Harris, your boss?"

"He was in love with Mary, I think. Never said it, but the way he watched her, I think he was jealous that she took it off for other men."

"Did you tell this to the police?"

"Oh, no. I don't have any proof, just a feeling in my gut, you know?"

"I still think you should report your suspicions. Let the police investigate and prove or disprove your theory."

"Oh, I don't know."

"Think about it," I said and moved on to casual conversation about the carnival and the weather.

Overall, it was a good talk. If other people could confirm this Bill thing, it would be something worth looking into. But even without her mentioning this to Chief Davis, I was sure he was already looking into that piece of human debris. It would be impossible for a guy like that to be near a murder and not be a suspect.

If others would say the same thing, I could report the possibility that she was killed by someone with romantic feelings toward her without mentioning names. Honestly, I didn't think that swine could have romantic feelings toward anyone, but I couldn't write in the paper that she was possibly killed by someone who wanted to fuck her. That was an obvious conclusion, that it was Bill or some other horny bastard who she wouldn't let stick it in her. My gut said it was one of the useless humans in the audience.

That isn't to say that everyone who attends a girl show is useless. Many upstanding citizens attend. But a large part of the crowd was, as it always is, older-looking men who likely work as dishwashers or mailmen and haven't been laid in twenty or so years. These dirty men have no job of any importance, no ambition, no wife, nothing.

They just go through their miserable lives, and their only happiness comes from a bottle or paying some woman to get naked. They are the kind of people who no one would miss if they died. "Hey, Charlie, you hear Jesse died?"

Charlie shrugs. "He was a worthless human being anyway. Pass the salt."

My gut told me that one of these worthless humans was the murderer.

I hung around the fairgrounds all afternoon and had some casual conversation with some of the carnies but learned nothing new. Later in the afternoon, I saw the police chief enter the lot. I approached him.

"Chief, sir," I called out.

He shook his head. "What do you want?"

"Nothing in particular. Just saying hi. So, what brings you back here so soon?"

"Police business."

"Well, sir—"

He cut me off. "I'm not telling you anything, so don't ask."

"I was just—"

He cut me off again. How rude.

"If you don't turn around and walk away, I'm going to haul you in. I have work to do."

"Okay, okay," I said as I put my hands up and walked away. I had a story to write. Spending time in jail wasn't going to help me get it done any quicker. When I was far enough away, I turned and watched Davis. He went to Bozo the Clown's door. Old Bozo answered and let him in.

Now we were getting somewhere. Why would he be talking to that deranged clown again so soon? Either Bozo knew something or he was a suspect.

Based on the little I knew, my hunch was the old man was a prime suspect. I lit a cigarette and waited.

When Davis emerged from the trailer, he didn't talk to anybody else. He just went to his car and left. It was time to see what I could find. It would be great for my career if I could find and report the smoking gun evidence before the cops found it. I decided to make another attempt to speak with the clown.

I knocked and the old clown opened the door just enough to stick his head out. He immediately asked, "What do you want?"

He acted like he didn't remember me from before so I began by telling him, "I'm a reporter for—"

"Can't talk now," he quickly said and slammed the door closed.

I knocked again but he remained quiet.

Next, I went over to try speaking to the owner of the carnival. As I approached his trailer, he happened to be stepping out of it. I ran up to catch him before he got away. "Excuse me, sir."

"What do you want?" he responded.

I could tell he was in a foul mood so tried to be as friendly to this man as possible. I hated to be this close to him again. He was a dumpy-looking man with a mixture of black and gray stubble that covered his face. And I could tell from the smell that he hadn't made a serious attempt to clean himself for a few days.

But I was a professional and was determined to be nice to this swine and learn what I could. I extended my hand to him. "I'd like to speak with you if I may."

"Sure, why not?" he said, ignoring my hand. "You're that reporter, right?"

"Yes, I am," I said.

"What do you want to know?"

"First, I'd like to offer my sympathy over what happened," I said, trying to get on his good side, but his response was just some ape sound. I moved on to my first question for him. "How long has the victim been working for you?"

"Fourteen years."

That seemed like well past the expiration date for a stripper. "Fourteen years?" I asked. "Strippers don't usually last that long, do they?"

"Hell, no. Girls come an' go every year. But not Mary. She was a good werker an' always happy to be here."

It was time to get more serious. "I was told that you were in love with her. Is this true?"

"Who told you that?"

"I can't reveal that."

"It ain't true. I liked her. She was a fine werker, but I don't go fer loose women like that. We fucked once years ago, but that was all."

"So you were just friends?" I asked.

"Yeah, just good friends."

"Was she romantically involved with anyone who works for you?"

"Not that I knows of. I hope not. I don't go fer cowerkers contortin' with each other like that." I knew what he meant so I didn't interrupt to tell him what he actually said. "We're always together so there's the occasional fuck, but if it gits serious they ga to go," he told me. "A bad breakup would be hell on us."

"That makes sense." I finished jotting down some notes then asked, "How would you describe the victim?"

"Tough broad. She was nice, loose, tough, loyal. Shit, it sounds like I'm describin' a Boy Scout, but she was all those things. I'll miss her."

I did not want to know about his experiences as a Boy Scout. I wrote down his description of her for reasons unknown to me. While I was doing this, he broke in.

"Listen, I need to be done with this."

"I understand," I told him. "Thank you for your time."

That evening I returned to the office to write up what I learned from my many interviews that day. When I was finishing my story for tomorrow's edition, my editor came up to my desk.

"Brian," he said.

"Yeah, Chuck, what do you want?"

"I just received a call about you."

"About me? What did I do?" Chuck could obviously tell from the look on my face that I thought I was in some kind of trouble or had pissed someone off. "This is good news," he quickly told me. Seems he had received a call from the editor for a large Cleveland paper. "They want to hire you to write up this carnival murder story for them."

This was good news.

"Are you okay with that?" I asked.

"As long as you want to." Of course I fucking wanted to. "It shouldn't interfere with your regular work since you're covering that story anyway," he added.

I tempered my enthusiasm in front of Chuck. I didn't want him knowing how eager I was to leave this dinky paper, but of course I would do it. "Sure, I'll do it."

"I'll let them know. Their editor will be in touch."

He went into his office, leaving me alone to think. This was a great opportunity for me, getting to write a story for a major paper. A few minutes later, I received the call. It was the Cleveland paper's editor. He briefly covered the basics: pay, rough word count, that sort of thing. Then he gave me some very exciting news. This would be the lead story, front page. He also said he had looked over some of my past work, was impressed, and gave me complete freedom over what to include in the story. I was thrilled. I was convinced that this would be my big break.

When the call finished, I sat back for a moment and

thought. Who could the killer be? If I could figure it out before the police, that could be huge for me. I thought back over my interviews. I thought the murderer was probably some loser in the crowd. If it was a carny, my first instinct was that it was the carnival's owner, Bill, but then I thought about it and realized there wasn't any evidence against him. My mind was probably going to him because he was such a wretched human being. He seemed like the kind of person who would do something like this. That, and the possibility of a sexual relationship between him and the woman killed, intrigued me. Maybe I was onto something? Damn it, not now. I stopped this train of thought. I didn't have any real evidence against him, and I couldn't sit here exploring possibilities all night. I had work to do, and I had to work with what I knew—with the known facts.

The story I had just written was geared toward locals, so I'd have to write up a different version for Cleveland. It didn't have to be too different since it wasn't like I was writing for a national publication. Cleveland was nearby—a short drive whenever I wanted to take in a professional baseball or football game. I'd just have to change the article a little. Then who knows, perhaps a national publication would come calling. I thought about how this would be my chance to move on to a major publication and cover real, important stories. I'd have to travel to cover many of these. I always liked working in other cities. I may have been a big fan of the country home idea, but I loved getting to chase stories in the big cities. I imagined myself, a year from now, chasing down stories in New York City or Washington, DC. A clear picture formed in my head of me sitting in some old, dark, Washington bar having a private conversation with some slimy politician who tells me that the communists have a secret plot to brainwash us through television and newspaper advertisements. At this point in the conversation, his lizard tongue extends from his mouth to grab a peanut out of a bowl. The image of him offering me a nut was clear as day when I suddenly realized that there wasn't time to hope and daydream now, I had a job to do. I flipped open my lighter, lit a cigarette, and got to it.

Chapter 14

Arianna Lewis,
Monday, November 2, 1953:

It was another restless night. With thoughts of Mary and the sounds of the wind blowing, it would have been tough to sleep, but adding Tina to that equation made it impossible. She talked through much of the night, not saying much, just wanting conversation—so she didn't feel alone. I was glad I could be there for her, but it was taking its toll on me. I wasn't getting any sleep because of it, and much of what Tina wanted to talk about was depressing, even when it wasn't about what happened to Mary.

Though we were on our second year working together, I had never known why she joined the carnival until she told me that night.

She said she had been desperate for money. "I needed it any way I could get it," she told me.

She joined about the time I did. She hoped to get a job with the Freak Show, but at the time, they already had a legless girl, Jenny, who left at the end of last year. Because Jenny was around, Bill suggested to Tina that she give stripping a try.

"That was like a punch in the gut," Tina said. "The thought of it made me sick, so I barged out of the office and went home, crying all the way. The worst part was that deep down I knew I had to consider it. I spent a night in the bathroom, vomiting. I was so sick over it. The next day I took the job."

All the time I had known Tina she had put on such a good front that I never realized how much she hated her job.

"Sometimes I still become sick after shows," she said after a pause. "I can't stand it, and I hate the men—hate them. I used to imagine myself married," she said while she wiped her eyes, "but now, I'd be happy if I never saw another man ever again. They all disgust me."

I felt so bad for her, but at the same time, the selfish part of me just wanted her to be quiet so I could get some sleep. I hated myself for it, but this is not what I wanted to talk about while we were still in shock over Mary's murder. Listening to Tina just made me feel worse.

I was so relieved when the sun came up, and hopeful I could find something to distract me from the pain around here. Unfortunately, the recent tragedy was visible on everyone's face. I socialized some with my friends here, but it didn't help my mood much at all.

A few of the carnies opened up their stands and made us some lunch. It began as a quiet meal time. The pain was building inside of me. As more and more carnies started to eat, some conversations began. I was finally getting my wish—friends were talking about casual, light topics and not the murder—but it didn't help me like I had thought it would. Listening to people be upset earlier, and Tina through the night, I think perhaps I just needed my turn to be sad and vent, but I didn't want to bring everyone back down, so I kept my feelings to myself.

After eating, I just wandered away and walked alone down the midway, looking at the still rides and closed attractions. I was delighted when I saw Brian, that cute reporter, enter the fairgrounds. I needed someone who would listen to me so I approached him. "Good morning," I said, even though it was actually around noon. "Hey, Arianna," he responded.

He appeared to be happy to see me. He asked how I was, which gave me a chance to talk about how bad I felt. During this, he placed his hand on my shoulder to comfort me. It felt nice. I told him about my fears that the person who did this was still out there.

He tried his best to reassure me. "Chief Davis will catch the killer," he told me.

He seemed confident when he said this. I did not share his confidence, but Brian was convinced the police chief would bring the murderer to justice. Brian's confidence made me feel better.

I hoped he was right. We were then both silent, just long enough for it to be awkward, until he said, "Well, I should get back to work."

"Oh, okay," I said, trying to hide my disappointment. I had hoped we could talk about something not related to my friend's death, something to take my mind off it, but that didn't happen. "I'll see you around."

"Bye, Arianna," he said and walked off.

Chapter 15

Bill Harris:

On Monday, I decided to take in the town. If I was goin' to be stuck here, I might as well see where I was stuck. I decided to walk there. Without the carnival to run, I had nothin' better to do.

It was a quiet little place. The main street was lined with shops an' eateries. A gazebo was in the middle o' the grass triangle between the streets. The people seemed to be out o' some Norman Rockefeller painting an' the soun' o' the nearby waterfall only added to the peaceful feelin' the place gave off. I'd have enjoyed myself if I weren' so fuckin' cole. It must o' been in the low ferties—not the place fer me.

I walked through the shops an' had a burger. The waitress who served it was one o' those uglies in lipstick.

It was a good enough meal 'spec fer some guy who kept lookin' at me. Maybe he was a sodomite. Kin' o' looked like he wanted me.

It was after lunch an' a bit o' walkin' that I seen somethin' amazin'. This retard boy was walkin' with a woman who appeared to be his ma. The boy was maybe seventeen. The fascinatin' thing 'bout him was his tiny face. His head was normal size but his eyes, nose, an' mouth covered such a small area in the center. It was uncanny. What an amazin' find. I could see the exhibit now: "The Boy with the Tiny Face."

I had to have him. But as I approached the 'tard, I paused. He had more wrong with him than the tiny face. He was clearly one o' those Down Syndrome kids an', from what little I observed, his ma seemed very protective o' him. My gut said she'd never go along with this. But on the other han', what else would a boy like that do? Become an accountant? It was clear this boy wouldn' have many options in life. I approached 'em.

"Excuse me," I said.

The boy remained silent.

"Yes?" the woman asked as she put her arm aroun' the boy's shoulder an' pulled him close—not a good sign.

"You have a very unique boy there. Is that your son?"

"Yes," she said, eyin' me suspiciously.

"Let me gi' to the point. Have you thought 'bout his future? I mean, what's a boy like that goin' to do?"

"Excuse me?"

"No offense. I just mean, you know how he is. How's he goin' to make a livin'? You won' be aroun' ferever."

"He is very bright," she shot back, obviously offended.

"I'm sure he is—fer one o' those."

At this point, he looked to her an' asked, "Who is this man?"

I put my han's on my knees, leaned down a little—the boy was maybe five feet, six inches—an' face to face, asked him, "How would you like to be in the carnival?"

"I like carnival—"

An' before he could continue his ma broke in. "We're leaving," the bitch said an' walked off, pullin' him along.

Poor kid. He had no future with her. She would take care o' him an' spoil him. Then one day she would die an' he would be lost. I offered the tiny-faced 'tard a chance to be someone. I shook my head in disgust an' walked on.

I had walked down the entire main street, crossed over, an' was walkin' back when I saw a broad that I thought would make a good stripper. I didn' approach her. We waited fer girls to come to us fer the kootch show. If you just go walkin' up to a girl on the street an' ask her if she wants to be a stripper, it usually don't go well. Actually, I wanted to approach her fer personal reasons. She was a cute chick of indiscriminate age with enormous juggs. As I was watchin' her, she walked into a shop. I didn' follow. I wasn' in the mood to werk fer sex.

I hadn' realized how long I'd been in town 'til a group o' little statutories passed me. School must have let out. It had been a good day an' I didn' have nothin' lef' to see so I slowly headed back to the fairgrounds.

I observed somethin' tha' took me aback durin' my return. I was passin' a wooded field while approachin' the fairgrounds when I noticed Gino in the woods walkin' to the road. I stepped behind a tree an' hid while watchin' him. Fear overtook me an', fer a brief moment, I became convinced that he was the murderer. As he came closer to the road, I noticed he was carryin' a shovel. My heart seemed to stop. I was extremely relieved when I realized that in his other han' he was carryin' the crapper from his trailer. The blood flowed back into my face. I guess that startle was what I deserved fer bein' so suspicious. The shovel had thrown me. Gino was usually one fer just dumpin' his waste in the middle o' the road, so it didn' immediately occur to me that he could be doin' somethin' so innocent. It was good to see he wasn' up to any funny business an' that he was finally buryin' his shit. I waited a moment, so he was far enough along that he wouldn' know I had been watchin' him, then started back to the fairgrounds.

Chapter 16

Tom Davis:

I spent Monday morning in town questioning random local citizens. I searched for persons who had been at the carnival Saturday night to ask if they noticed anything unusual.

Of course, this buckshot approach did not produce any results other than an amusing story about a man who tried to attack Bozo in his dunk tank. That was fine. I really didn't have high expectations of finding anything important. I just wanted a better picture of the night. This would help me as the investigation continued. Also, it was impossible to predict which long-shot approach might actually produce results, so I needed to try everything I could think of.

I also put a notice in the local paper. It read:

> *Seeking Information Related to Fair-grounds Murder. If anyone noticed anything suspicious at the fairgrounds last Saturday night (October 31) please contact Police Chief Davis.*

This was followed by the station address and phone number. This was necessary because I had so little to go on. If it wasn't a carny who did this, I would need a lucky break if I had any chance of finding the killer.

I did not know if I was dealing with a crazed local citizen or an angry or insane coworker. Judging by the fact that the victim had been naked and from her position, I assumed there was a sexual element. The coroner and medical examiner found no signs of rape or sexual intercourse, but the way she was found—naked, face down, with her hand between her legs—did suggest she was engaged in foreplay or preparing for sex. If it was a rape attempt, the act was never completed. It might be someone she rejected, or someone who realized her motel room key scam was, in fact, a scam. If it was a carny, Guglielmo and Radowski topped the list. But if either was guilty, they did a hell of a job leaving themselves and the crime scene evidence free. I didn't find anything linking them to the scene, and neither did detective Perry. That Radowski had the victim's cat was suspicious, but if he did murder her why would he take her cat when he left the scene? If he was the killer it would be idiotic to keep something that tied him so closely to the victim. On the other hand, maybe he knew someone saw him with her—or at least knew that was a possibility—and kept the cat to explain that. If she did give him the cat to watch, I wish she had told him the reason why. Maybe the answer was in why he had the cat? Was she planning to meet some man and wanted the cat out of the way? A planned sexual encounter with a fellow carny or local townsperson?

I looked over my interviews again, hoping I'd see something I previously missed. I called Perry to ask if he had looked over the interviews yet. He said he had, but could draw no clear conclusions from them. "It's my opinion that the guilty party is the clown Radowski, or girl-show operator Guglielmo, or the owner Harris," he told me.

"What makes you suspect them?"

"A hunch."

"Any reason that you can articulate?"

"It was most likely someone she knew, right?"

"That's usually the case, yes," I answered.

"She knew them."

There was a long pause as I waited—expecting him to say more. When I realized he had completed his thought, I said, "That is true, she did know them," and after gathering my thoughts said, "but she knew everyone at the carnival."

"But one was angry at her, and there are possible

romantic interests with the other two—I mean them with her, not each other," he said, followed by an odd, fake-sounding laugh. "You should focus on them, not that you'll find anything. The case will most likely never be solved," he added bluntly.

I knew the chances were high that the case would go unsolved, but I did not understand why Perry felt it important to keep reminding me of this. His lack of caring irritated me immensely.

After the call, I tried to put Perry out of my mind. I looked over the reports from the coroner and medical examiner again, even though there wasn't much in them. The lack of evidence in the report from the lab was stunning, and the only useful information in the medical examiner's report was the approximate time of death and that the lack of hesitation cuts in the stab wound showed she was most likely murdered as opposed to having committed suicide.

I spent the rest of the day working the phones. I took hours. First, I made calls to learn as much as I could about the pasts of Mary, Bill, and Guglielmo then to research the history of the carnival and find out if they had any past troubles associated with them that no one had mentioned. I found reports of the typical carnival scams, but nothing on this level.

Chapter 17

Brian Stockton:

Early in the morning, I awoke and immediately went to and opened my door. On the step were two papers, our town paper and the Cleveland one that I luckily already subscribed to. I picked it up. What a fucking kick in the crotch. There was another murder, somewhere. The headline read, "Ohio Farmer Murdered in Home." Of all the lousy luck. I couldn't catch a break.

I scanned the page for my story. When I finally found it, I became even more pissed. It was edited down to almost nothing. Those fucking cocksuckers, didn't they know a good story when they saw it? Who gave a shit about some boring farmer?

This story had everything: strippers, freaks, murder,

and mystery. What the fuck was wrong with them?

I quickly dressed and hurried to the office, hoping my editor had heard some explanation for this. I barged into his office without knocking. "Chuck."

"Brian, knock damnit."

"Have you seen the paper?"

"Of course I've seen it. I check every issue."

"Not ours, this." I threw it down on his desk.

"Oh, that. Yeah, I saw it."

"Look what they did with my article."

It really couldn't even be called an article at this point. I was now not only indignant about the piece, but angry that Chuck didn't care more.

"Those are the breaks."

"The breaks?" What the fuck was wrong with him? "What the fuck is wrong with you? There's nothing left. A chimp could have written that. I'm embarrassed having my name by that tiny blurb." He shrugged. "Chuck, they cut me out for a fucking farmer," I growled. "Who gives a shit about him?"

"He's a local, Brian. Your story was about an outsider, someone no one here knows or cares about."

"That's bullshit."

"It's the truth. Now, if one of those carnies had killed a local, then you'd have your headline."

"Shit."

He was correct. What more could I say? My only hope now was that it was a local who did the killing, otherwise this story probably wouldn't make it anywhere. It suddenly didn't look like the opportunity I hoped it would be. My first instinct was to go get a drink, but I knew sulking about the situation wouldn't help.

I went to the fairgrounds to find out if there was any breaking news. I exited my car and lit a cigarette. I was humming a song. It was a song that had played on the radio that morning and it had been stuck in my head since.

The problem was that I couldn't remember most of the lyrics and it was driving me crazy. I kept hearing one small part over and over. And was even singing the piece of crap under my breath: "Istanbul was Constantinople. Now it's Istanbul not Constantinople. B…fuck what's next? Not Constantinople. I don't know and somethin' 'bout the Turks."

Fuck it. I hated the Four Lads anyway. Why couldn't I forget their damn song?

I entered the carnival lot. As I walked to Bill's trailer, Arianna came up to me. "Good morning," she said.

"Hey, Arianna." She looked lovely. Seeing her was the bright spot of what was so far a shit morning. "How are you today?" I asked, which as soon as I said it I realized was dumb question. Her friend was recently brutally murdered. How did I think she would be?

"Oh, could be better," she replied, which was preferable to her telling me I was a dumbass for asking the question.

"I'm sure it has been tough." I couldn't believe that's the genius comment I said next. This morning was not going well.

"Yes, and not just the losing a friend," she said. "It all has me concerned. I don't feel right."

"Yeah, I can imagine it's been difficult."

I put a hand on her shoulder to try to offer some comfort. I knew my words weren't helping. I quickly realized the hand on the shoulder was a mistake too. After how awkward I had been acting, she probably thought I was hitting on her or something. I'm sure it came across as slimy. With all these thoughts going through my head, I tried listening to her as best as I could.

"The person who did this is still out there and can do it again at any time," she said. "They could be one of my friends, someone I trust."

I tried offering her some hope. "Chief Davis will catch the killer."

She sighed. "I hope so."

"He will. We don't see eye to eye on everything, but he's good at his job. I'm sure he will find the guilty party."

She smiled at me. It was a cute smile. I hated myself for noticing that while she was going through so much pain.

"Well, I hope he solves this soon," she said, continuing the conversation.

"He's a determined man," I said and then praised

Chief Davis and told her he probably already knew who the killer was, but that he just needed to gather enough evidence to convict. I didn't really believe this, but I knew it could be true, and it made her feel better. After telling her this, there was a moment of silence. I sensed she didn't want to talk right now, and probably thought I was acting a bit odd, so I searched for a way to end this. Finally I simply said, "Well, I should get back to work."

"Oh, okay," she said, and probably to be polite added, "I'll see you around."

"Bye, Arianna." I walked away and headed to see that slob Bill.

While I was on my way to see him, a carny came running up to me. "Hey, stop," he called out. I immediately recognized him as the doctor in the brainless Betty exhibit. "You're the reporter, right?" he asked me.

"I am," I told him. "I'm Brian."

"My name is Will. I have something very important to tell you."

From the look in his eyes, I thought it must be serious, so I said, "Let's go over here so we'll be out of the way."

"Good thinking," he said as I took him to an unoccupied corner of the backyard where I hoped we could speak undisturbed.

"Go ahead," I said as I lit up a Fatima. "What do you know?"

He nervously looked around and then back at me.

"I'm glad to have the chance to talk. What I have to say needs to get out. This thing, it's a big cover up. It goes to the top."

I took a drag off my cigarette. "Go on."

He looked around again then looked right into my eyes. "They're here." He stared as if he expected this to mean something to me.

"Who?" I finally asked. "Who's here?"

He pointed to the sky. "Them. They're here."

"Birds?" I asked sarcastically, knowing that isn't what he meant.

"Aliens."

"Aliens are here?"

"Yes. The government knows all about it. They've talked to them. Big secret." He quickly looked around again then back to me. Then his voice dropped to a whisper. "They made the bomb."

"Aliens made the bomb?" I played along as I tried to figure out if he was serious.

"Yes, and they told us to use it. It was their idea to kill the Japs like that. They won the war for us. We've been in their debt ever since."

By the way he whispered and nervously and repeatedly glanced around, I came to the conclusion that this man believed what he was telling me. I played along. I knew this would be the easiest way to get rid of him. "So we're in their debt? So what?"

"Don't you see? It's time for them to collect."

"Collect? How? What do they want?"

"The complete collapse of our government. They've already planted high-ranking officials in the governments of each of the forty-six states."

I didn't have the heart to tell him there were forty-eight states.

"Once they've destroyed us, the Russians will come in and turn us into slaves."

I took a deep breath to keep myself from laughing. "They want to make us slaves for the Russians?"

"Exactly."

"And why are they working on behalf of the Russians?"

"The Russians and aliens are both atheists. It's a damned atheist/communist plot. Don't you see? The Godless stick together. Commies help commies."

"The aliens are communist too?" I asked.

"Of course they are—all atheists are communists. It's part of their religion and philosophy."

"I didn't know that," I said as seriously as I was able.

"Now you know. That's the bond the aliens and Russians share."

"So, why tell me?"

"You're with the press," he told me. "You can break this story. It's our only way. Mass revolt. It's our only hope."

"Don't tell anybody about this," I said with as straight a face as possible. "I'll make some inquiries and do what I can."

"Be careful," he said grimly. "They won't hesitate to take you out."

"I'll be careful."

"Good luck." He held out his hand. "Good luck," he repeated as he shook my hand with obvious respect for the task he thought I was going to take on. Then he walked away.

I spent another hour or so at the fairgrounds, first looking for Bill, but not finding him, and then failing at another attempt to get Bozo the Clown to speak to me. After him, I ran across a dirty looking little man. "Excuse me, sir," I said as I approached him.

"What do you want?"

"I'm Brian, a reporter with the local paper."

"Go fuck yourself." He spit on the ground and stomped off.

I quickly ran up to the next guy I saw. "Who is that?" I asked him as I pointed to the man who had just told me to go fuck myself.

"That's Gino."

"The kootch show operator?"

"Yeah, that's him."

I shook my head. I had wanted to speak with Gino but, judging from that reaction, didn't think I'd have any luck getting him to tell me anything. I turned my attention to the man I was now speaking with. His name was Marshall. He was the midget who worked as the barker for the kootch show. After him, I talked to Sam who ran the Devil's Lair. From them I did not learn anything new. In fact, Will's alien theory was the most newsworthy thing I learned at the fairgrounds that morning. Before leaving, I helped a group of carnies pick up Ingrid. Seems she wanted some fresh air, stepped out of her trailer, slipped, and fell in the mud. She had not exaggerated when we spoke yesterday. It took three of us to help her stand.

Chapter 18

Bill Harris,
Tuesday, November 3, 1953:

Another mornin' in fuckin' Ohio. Son o' a bitch. I had me some coffee then walked the grounds to check on everythin'. Everyone seemed to be holdin' up fine—a little tense an' pissed fer sure, but as well as one would figure. I went back to my trailer, sat alone at my desk, an' had some more coffee. Took some time to think.

I wondered if I was doin' the right thing in keepin' everyone here. There wasn' too much complainin', but the year was done an' everyone wanted to be home. I was jus' tryin' to do what's right an' help the police. I don't think that copper had much help. One o' his deputies who had been here seemed as useless as tits on a cow. Whatever the police asked, I tried to do. O' course we all wanted justice fer Busty…well, 'spec the guy who done it, I guess. But Busty was a special girl, an' I wanted to be helpful. But fer how long I didn' know. I couldn' keep everyone here ferever. I decided to give it a few more days then tell the chief we was leavin'. What could he say? Had to understan'.

The thing was, I wasn' sure he'd fin' nothin' here. I mean, maybe it was someone here, I don't know, but it was just as likely, if not more, that it was a town folk. That's the danger o' the girl show. Some guys git horny an' want stuff, an' when they don't git it, some git angry. It ain't often but it happens. An' Busty also had her hotel key scam. I've told her she should stop that, but she kept it up. I werried it could lead to somethin' like this, but what was I goin' to do, git rid o' the girl show? Couldn' do that. The hootchie-kootchie girls bring in enough money to choke a chicken. Fuck it all.

I sat aroun' fer a while more just thinkin'. I had owned this carnival fer fourteen years. In tha' time we've had to deal with occasional deaths. There were always some with us who weren't the most responsible people in the world. We've had kootch show girls with drug problems, an' some o' our deformed performers have health problems, so deaths happened. As near as I could figure, we've lost seven carnies before Mary, not countin' those who left then died. My first year here we lost a flunky who got drunk an' died in a river. A showgirl died from a drug overdose. A barker died on the job o' a heart attack. Two human oddities died o' health reasons related to their deformities. Alfred, who ran a BB gun gallery we used to have, died o' cancer, an' we lost a pinhead who got hit by a train—what a mess. But we ain't never had nothin' like this. A murder was different, 'specially when it might have been one o' our own who did it. I wasn' sure how it would affect the group an' their ability to stay together.

I got up an' walked the backyard again. Since there was no trouble, I thought I'd go into town to git lunch. I was havin' the urge fer some beef brains. Thought I'd go to the butcher, git me some, an' bring 'em back here. As I was walkin' out, I saw the cop car. I looked aroun' but didn' see him. Thought it best fer me to fin' him, tell him my decision to leave in a few days. Best he knew that. I looked aroun' but couldn' fin' him. Where could he be? I headed toward Otto's trailer. We was all suspectin' him a little, so just a hunch the police chief might be too. As I approached, the chief was walkin' away from Otto's trailer. "Chief."

"Yes, Bill?"

We reached each other.

"Um, I been thinkin'. You know I can't keep every-one here ferever."

"Yes, I know, and I appreciate you staying and how cooperative you and everybody that works for you has been."

"The thing is we gots to leave."

"What?"

"Not now, but in a few days. Can't keep 'em here all winter."

"But, Bill, you want the killer caught, don't you?"

"Yes, o' course."

"Then I need more time. Things are not unfolding as fast as I had hoped."

"Try puttin' the foot on the other shoe. What would you do if you were me?"

There was a long silence. I must have ga to him. He was thinkin' 'bout what I said—thinkin' my position over.

"Just give me a little more time," he said finally. "I promise if no progress is being made soon, I'll let you go."

"Well—"

He cut me off. "I'd hate to have to get a court order forcing you to stay."

"All right. Do what you need."

"Thank you."

"Bye." He walked off.

Damn it to fuckin' hell. No use pissin' 'bout it. My stomach was growlin'. I'd feel better when I got my brains. I was so hungry. Suddenly I realized that the cop was probably fixin' to go to town. I ran after him to grab a ride. Nope, shit, he wasn' goin' to town. Back to walkin'. I used the doniker then left fer town.

Chapter 19

Brian Stockton:

Tuesday morning, I was still on the front page in town but the situation was much worse in Cleveland. My story was again cut down to almost nothing and, this time, stuck in the middle of the paper. I did get a small glimmer of hope for the story when I received a call from a national magazine. The murder and circumstances intrigued them, but the call abruptly ended with them just leaving a number and asking me to contact them "if something new happened." This was discouraging. Well, if something did happen, I wanted to be the one to write the story—not just be a source. I was determined not to just keep on the case, but also to learn as much about the carnies as I could. This was an interesting group. They could be a selling point to taking this thing national. I wouldn't let this story slip away like I did when that dope smoking Arab dry cleaner got busted for that shit he did with those Indian remains in El Paso in '48.

I headed to the fairgrounds to conduct more interviews with the carnies. When I arrived, I saw that asshole who ran the place and, not wanting to talk to him, I approached the closest person I saw and started a conversation. The man's name was Jake. He ran a stand where he fried cheese. Came from Peoria. Not much else to say about Jake. He was a pretty uninteresting guy, from what I could tell, didn't witness anything on the night of the murder, and didn't have any thoughts about who might have done it. I quickly moved on.

Next, I interviewed Gary. I recognized him right away but couldn't remember where I had seen him. In response to me questioning him about this, he popped his eyeballs out of their sockets.

"Oh yes, Popeye."

Those were some crazy eyes he had. Good for him. Without them, I could maybe see him pumping gas, but not doing much else. Definitely not a good deal like he had now. You could get up early for some nine to five job that you couldn't stand, working your ass off for little pay, or pop your eyeballs out of their sockets for curious spectators. I'd rather do that than pump gas all day, flip burgers, or work in a bank.

No thanks to that.

Anyway, I interviewed Gary. He didn't give me any-thing I could use.

Next, I spoke with a stripper who went by the name Juggs Mackenzie on and off the stage. She looked much worse up close than on stage and sounded even worse than that. She smoked constantly and had the voice of a woman who had been at it nonstop for a hundred and fif-ty years.

"Have a seat," she said to me in her rough voice as we sat in two plastic chairs that were in front of her trail-er.

"Thank you," I said and sat. "How are you doing?"

"I feel sick over everything."

"I'm sorry. I know losing a friend like that must be rough."

"Hell yeah."

"I'll try to make this quick then."

"No need to hurry. I can feel shitty with or without you. Makes no difference to me."

"How long have you been with the carnival?"

"With this one, five years, but I worked for a few others before that."

"Same job with all of them?"

"Yep. Easy money."

"Do you like it?"

"Hell no, I hate the noise of the carnival and taking my clothes off for people, but it pays and I have no other skills. I needed to do something to get myself away."

"To get away from what?" I asked.

"My home. I was sixteen when I took my first job and made my escape. Had an uncle who had been living with us for a few years. I developed young, and he noticed. Oh, honey, did he notice."

"So he abused you?" I don't know why I asked that question since I knew the answer.

"Started touching me when I was fourteen and soon was doing more. Told me no one would believe me if I told and of all the trouble I'd get in for spreading lies. Finally I just picked up and left."

It surprised me how up-front she was about her life. I didn't know how to respond to her. All I came up with was, "I'm sorry."

"Sorry for what? You didn't do it. That's life. And anyway, I've got a job and friends here. I've made the best of it."

"That's a good attitude."

"What else can I do? I get along fine. I don't know what I'll do when this job ends. I'm already past my prime, but I don't know what I'm going to do next, so I'll milk it for as long as I can."

I didn't know how to respond to her life story. Her life depressed me so I decided to move the interview along.

"How well did you know the victim?"

"Good. We were close. Even vacationed together last winter. Went to Paramus."

"When was the last time you saw her?"

"During her last day. Just said 'hi' in passing."

"So you didn't see her during the show?"

"No, didn't bump into each other. Our shows are spread out. Guess Gino doesn't want to put the two oldest girls on back to back," she said with a hoarse laugh.

"Did you witness anything suspicious that night?"

"Nothing."

"Any ideas who might have done this?"

"Not a clue, honey. Of course I've had my suspicions of certain people here, but I try not to think about."

"Can you tell me who you suspect?"

"No, honey. I don't want to throw out names. I really know nothing about it. Nothing I know is based on anything important."

"What's it based on?"

"Just past stuff."

"Like interactions between other carnies and the victim?"

"Oh no, no, nothing like that. Past crimes, well, accusations really."

Now we were getting somewhere.

"What kind of accusations?" I asked.

"Look, honey, I really shouldn't be telling you this, but Otto Radowski has been accused of things. No one really knows much about it, but years ago we were drinking together one night and he told me he had been accused of molesting a young boy. He said it wasn't true and cried about it."

"Do you know any details about the crime?"

"No, honey, he didn't give me any, and no one else knows. I mean, some people know he was accused of something, but no one really knows what."

"I see."

"Please don't report that, and if you ask anyone about it, keep my name out of it."

"I will. I understand," I said.

"Thank you," she said.

I had nothing else to ask. "Thank you for your time."

I interviewed a few others: Charlene, known as "Tiger Girl," Amy, a charming but seemingly cold Black stripper, and the Wolfman. I learned nothing new, and no one was able to add to the Radowski molestation story.

After these interviews, I had the fortunate sighting of Otto Radowski walking toward the back lot. I ran up to him. "Excuse me, Mr. Radowski," I called out. "I'd like to ask you a few questions."

"No, not now," he said and kept walking.

I decided to get to the point. "Mr. Radowski, what can you tell me about allegations that you molested a young boy."

"Ahhhhh!" he screamed and ran off.

I guess if I were accused of something like that, I wouldn't want to talk about it either. Next, I approached a guy I wish I hadn't. He appeared to be in his mid-fifties, was of an average build, with a mix of light brown and gray hair. He wore blue jeans, a red and black plaid flannel shirt, a tan jacket, and a tan flat cap.

"Hey, excuse me, sir," I called out as I approached him.

"Yes?"

"I'm a reporter for the local paper. I'd like to ask you a few questions."

"About the murder?"

"Yes, that and about yourself. I'm trying to get to know everyone, get a feel for the environment."

"'kay. Whadda wanna know?"

"We'll start with the crime. Did you know the victim well?"

"That depends. Whadda mean well?"

"Were you friends with her?"

"I liked her jus' fine."

"Did you spend much time together, or just bump into her once and a while?"

"No."

"Um…" I stopped myself from trying to get him to expand and moved on. "Okay. Do you know what happened on Saturday night?"

"I washed my clothes in the sink."

"I mean do you know anything about the murder?"

"She was killed."

"Anything else?"

"It rained."

"Anything else about the murder?"

"Jus' what I was told."

"And what were you told?"

"That she was killed."

I don't know why I continued, but I did. "Do you know of any reason why someone might have wanted to kill her?" I asked.

"No."

"Do you know of anyone that might have wanted to kill her?"

"No."

I could see I wasn't going to learn anything about the murder from him so I moved on. "So, what do you do here?"

"I run the merry-go-round."

"And you are?"

"The guy who runs the merry-go-round."

"I mean, what is your name?"

"Buddy."

At the top of my note page I wrote, "Buddy who runs the merry-go-round." I continued questioning him for reasons I never figured out. "How long have you been here?"

"'Bout a week."

"You've only been with the carnival for a week?"

"No, here, this place."

"How long have you worked for the carnival?"

"Ten years."

"Why did you want this job?"

"I ran a merry-go-round for another carnival before."

"I mean, why did you choose to become a carny?"

"I dunno."

"There must be some reason why you went to work for your first carnival."

"Yes."

"And that reason was?"

"I needed a job."

I paused then decided against continuing. I extended my hand. "Thank you for your time, Buddy."

"No problem."

I needed a break before talking to any more carnies so I decided to go town. As I was heading to my car, I saw Chief Davis parking. I intended to make the police station my next stop, so this saved me some time. I arrived at his car door as he was exiting. "Hello, Chief."

"What do you want?"

I looked around to make sure no one was around. "What do you know about Otto Radowski's past?" I asked.

"Anything in particular you want to know?"

"Sex pervert allegations."

"I thought you might be asking about that. I've been told, from the sheriff of Radowski's hometown, that the kid lied about Radowski."

"What does he base his opinion on?"

"The boy was a known liar—which as a man now he still is—and his story kept changing."

"Sounds like a bullshit claim then."

"Yes, it does."

"Thanks, Chief," I said, disappointed that this potential lead now seemed to be nothing.

"You're welcome," he responded.

I walked to my car and lit a cigarette.

Chapter 20

Arianna Lewis:

I spent Monday night with Tina. She was too frightened to be alone and still convinced Otto was the one who killed Mary. I thought she was way off base with her suspicions of him. He was odd, but I never considered him dangerous.

Her fear of him saddened me. It had taken so little to convince her.

The truth is that everything about this place made me uncomfortable. Tuesday I tried walking around and talking to some of my friends. I saw Betty alone, looking at the ground and kicking rocks. I figured she wanted to be alone, but at that moment she looked up, saw me, smiled, and waved.

I walked over. "Hey Betty, how you doing?"

"I'm doing just…" She shrugged.

"Same here." After a momentary pause I asked, "What are your plans for the winter?"

"Looking for a new job."

"You're leaving the carnival?"

"I can't stay working for him."

"Bill?"

"Not after what he did to Mary."

Her accusation surprised me. "You think Bill killed her?" I asked.

"Oh, yes. I knew he was dangerous."

"Did you see anything?"

"No. I just know, you know?"

I thought she let her fears get the better of her, but I just nodded. "Yeah, sure." This wasn't a conversation that was going to help me feel any better, so I tried to change it. "Will you try to get a job with another carnival?"

"I don't know. Maybe. Why do you think Bill did it?" She'd just accused him and now she was asking me about his motive?

"I…um…don't know," was all I could say.

"I think he was just mad about something. I don't know what."

"I don't know." Then I said, "I'm going to get something to drink."

"Okay, yeah," Betty responded.

I began to walk off.

"Toodles," she added as I made my escape.

I went up to Adrian, who was sitting in his open stand. I dropped down a nickel and two pennies. "Could I get a Coke?"

He looked up. "Oh, hi, Arianna. Yeah, sure." He grabbed a bottle out of the cooler and handed it to me with one hand while picking up the money with his other. "Fun place today, huh?" he said.

"Tell me about it."

He leaned close to me. "Who do you think did it?" he asked.

"I try not to think about it."

"Yeah, yeah, I can understand that. Do you want to know who I think is guilty?"

"To be honest, no. I'd rather not talk about that."

"Yeah, I can understand that. It's depressing knowing someone here killed Mary, and horrible to think that it was probably someone she knew and trusted. That they stuck a knife in her is awful. That's so up close and personal. It's such a horrible way to go."

At that moment, Amy came over to buy a soda pop. I used that as an excuse to get away and waved good-bye to Adrian. I tried socializing more, but it wasn't a good experience. No matter who I spoke with, they just served as a reminder of the murder. Perhaps someday I would get past this, but not today. This depressed me. I liked them all, but didn't want to see any of them, even Tina. She was being too clingy. I understood that she wasn't dealing with this well, but I was in pain too. I decided to tell her I would spend the coming night alone. She needed to cope with her fears, and I needed to try to get a full night's sleep, not another night of having my fears and stress intensified by hers.

I found her sitting on the merry-go-round platform. "Tina," I called out as I approached.

"Hi," she said softly.

"Can we talk?" I asked as I sat down next to her.

"Sure. About what?"

"Tonight. I think we ought to spend it away from each other."

She stiffened. "We can't be alone. What if Otto comes for one of us."

"Nothing is going to happen. Not now." I tried to think of reasons to comfort her, but all I could come up with was, "Too many people watching now. Whoever did this won't try again, not now."

"I suppose so," she said, "but I really need someone. I can't take feeling like this," she said as her eyes filled with tears.

This hurt me. I already felt bad for telling her this, like I was being a bad friend and selfish person by not being there for her, but I also needed to be there for myself.

"Tina, we just end up talking about things that make us both worry. It's not helping either of us."

"But—" she said but stopped.

I waited a couple of seconds and she didn't continue, so I told her, "I need my sleep and you need yours. The only way either of us will get any is to spend the night alone." She still looked concerned, so I added, "We're going to have to spend the night alone at some point."

"You're right," she said quietly. "I know you are. I'm just scared."

She looked up at me. I knew what she wanted. I embraced her. "Things will get better," I told her as we hugged.

She seemed to understand that at some point she would need to deal with this on her own. I hoped this would begin the healing process for her and that she would be able to sleep alone. And I needed my sleep and a night without hearing her talk about Otto. Everybody's suspicions upset me. Most of the people here had their own theory of who was guilty, and while a few thought it was a local stranger, most of those here suspected it was one of their former friends. I heard the names of at least ten of my friends and coworkers as being the guilty one from other friends. The murder, the lack of trust, it all made me sick. I didn't want to be around these people any longer. I just wanted to get away from here.

I walked over to the carnival games, hoping to distract myself from my painful thoughts. I opened up Knock Down a Killer Clown, placed a bunch of balls on the counter, took one ball in my hand, and went around to the outside. I eyed the first scary clown and took aim.

The throw was high and wide. I grabbed another ball. This next throw bounced off the railing right below the clown I aimed for. I took another ball, stopped, and stared at that scary clown and his wild hair. I threw and nailed it. I quickly grabbed another ball, took a small step to my right, and threw. I knocked the next one down. I repeated this action and knocked over a third. Now I was on a roll so I kept going. I knocked down the next three in quick succession and was quite proud of myself. Then I threw at the seventh clown—the last in the row—and missed to the left.

"Ah." I put my hands on my hips and looked to the sky. Now I had a goal. Get seven—knock down an entire row without a miss.

I went inside the booth and reset the clowns in the top row. Then I picked up the balls and laid them out on the counter. My next two tries to knock down seven didn't go well. First, I hit three in a row before failing, then I only hit one before the next miss. On my ensuing pass, after hitting two in a row, I missed on number three. I turned around in disappointment. My only thought was knocking down those damn clowns, but then I started focusing on the empty carnival I was looking at, and my mind turned back to the thoughts that consumed me earlier. It was especially stressful not knowing how long we would be here. I didn't even know if the police had the power to make us stay or if it was simply a request. I suppose it did not matter. We all wanted the killer caught and were willing to sacrifice until that was accomplished. I just hoped it would be solved soon. I wanted to go home.

Things were quiet Tuesday evening. No one was much in the mood for talking, so I just wandered around the fairgrounds alone for a bit and tried to think about things that were not depressing. I was looking forward to seeing my family in Kansas soon and imagined myself going out with that cute reporter Brian. I tried distracting myself this way, but it was impossible to go too long without thinking of what happened. There was a pain and hurt that would not go away.

All of the stress made me want to retire early and spend the evening alone. There wasn't much to do in my trailer except read, and it was difficult to concentrate on that with all that was on my mind. Still, I was thankful for this alone time. It gave me a chance to grieve for Mary. She had so much life still ahead. And it was such a violent death. I couldn't begin to imagine the fear and pain she had to endure. The thought of it made me sick.

Thinking of her also brought out fear. The murderer was still out there somewhere, and there were noises outside that gave me an unpleasant feeling. I knew it was only the wind but, considering recent events, it was a spooky sound. Its steady whistle kept my nerves on edge.

Suddenly there was a bang on the outer side of one of my walls. I thought maybe the wind had blown something into it, but I did not know. Whatever it was it made me jump. My heartbeat raced and I turned the lights off. Slowly and nervously, I moved to the window. I took a deep breath then drew the blind. I couldn't see anything outside.

Then suddenly someone popped up and stared right at me. I screamed. The person in the dark raised their hands as if telling me to be quiet. As I backed away, I made out the face in the moonlight. It was Gino. This did not make me feel any better, since it could have been him who murdered poor Mary. In my panic, I feared the worst. I didn't say anything. As I backed away, he disappeared.

There was a knock at the door. I stood silent, scared stiff. "Lewis, open up," Gino called out.

"What do you want?" I yelled as I moved to the kitchen counter to grab a knife.

"I was just checking on you," he said as I grabbed the knife.

"I'm fine," I responded sharply. "Why are you checking on me?"

He was eerily quiet for a long moment. The only sounds I could hear were my heavy breathing, my heart racing, and the wind outside.

"I was worried about you," he finally said. "I thought the man who got Mary might be afta you, doll."

He offered no further explanation and I didn't ask. He had me so frightened that I just wanted him to go away.

"I'm fine," I said again.

"Glad to hear it."

Then all was silent. I didn't know if he left or not. I sat on my bed for I don't know how long with the knife in my hand. I fell asleep holding it.

Chapter 21

Otto Radowski:

I tried to start taking my life back Tuesday. On Monday, old Otto mostly moped around on my own. When I went outside, people acted strange and quiet. Of course. How else should they act after the loss of friend Mary? We was all sad. But now was a new day, and Otto wanted life to start coming back. Get things back to how they were, minus Mary, of course, but people come and go, that's life, but there's still so many familiar faces here. Things can be normal again, Otto thought. That's what I wanted.

I hated how different things seemed. I knew life would go on if we just pulled together, and now I was determined to help with that. I went outside to start our recovery but my friends were no help with that, they were not. I saw Erik and Betty sitting and talking. Betty stood up and walked away so I decided to talk to Erik. I walked up to him and sat in the folding chair Betty had been in.

"Hiya, Erik. How you doing?"

"All right. Haven't been doing anything different than I'd be doing at home, so I can't complain."

"I see. That's good. Yeah, I like being here so I can be around friends. Hate when we break for winter. Well, don't hate at first. Little break good, you know, to get away. But then Otto miss friends, want friends, want break to be over, want to be back on job razzing marks. Fun being Bozo. Lots of fun. It's too bad we can't keep working while we're here. Or maybe we can. We're here already, so why not? Are we allowed to open again? Maybe I should ask Bill—"

"I want to be alone for a while," Erik cut in as he stood up.

He walked away. Otto can understand people wanting to be alone, but I think Erik lied 'cause I see him later not alone.

Then Otto saw Amy and walked up to her. "Heya, Amy. How you doing?"

"I'm so-so, Otto," she said. "Ready to leave here. How are you holding up?"

"Oh, you know, not well. Mary was so good."

"She was."

"Yessum," I said. "Good person, good heart. I feel lucky to, you know. Old Otto been here a long time.

Knew lots of people. Like Most. But Mary special." I thought of her and smiled. "I remember when she first started. I met her and Dan the Skeleton Man at the same time. Dan was before your time. He was skinny—real skinny. When I say skinny—I mean skinny. That's why they call him skeleton man, because he skinny. That was his act. Skinny guy. Funny guy. He used to love oatmeal. He one time—"

"You're boring me," Amy cut in suddenly and tramped off.

Otto stunned for moment and eyes tear up. I told myself to be a man. This all has strange effect on people, and some will act weird or rude. Yes, they will. So I wiped my eyes and continued on. Problem was everyone seemed distant. From afar, I'd see them and they looked like they were doing fine, talking and stuff, but whenever I tried to talk to someone, it wasn't that way. Maybe some of them know how close I was to Mary and feel bad for me, but I had bad feeling that some think Otto the guy who killed Mary.

I tried to make feeling go away and walk around more and talk to more people. I tried to show them all is the same old Otto and things can go back to being like they was, but it does no good. Maybe it was too soon for this, I thought. I decided to try again the next day. As I was walking to the back lot some guy came up to me. "Excuse me, Mr. Radowski, I'd like to ask you a few questions."

"No, not now," I said and kept moving. I didn't want to talk to outsiders about this stuff, but he followed.

"Mr. Radowski, what can you tell me about allegations that you molested a young boy."

"Ahhhhh!" Otto screamed and ran back to my trailer. Quickly got in and close door. How he know that? Oh damn. I was already sad and gonna tear up because no one want to talk, and now this. Why did these things get said? Hurt me. Oh. I groaned in pain, I did. Fell to the floor in pain. Was there curled up for long time.

For the rest of the day Otto cried alone. Oh, did I cry, for hours and hours. When stop I finally did, I looked outside and saw it was night. Well, I knew I must try to sleep.

Sad as I was, I had more control over myself than on previous nights, so, for the first time in many years, I said a nightly prayer I used to say every night when I was little Otto. Since then Otto still talked to God most nights, but our relationship had grown more casual. But now this old prayer was what Otto needed. I thought for a moment and the words came back into my head. Happy I remembered it.

I kneeled next to my bed and folded my hands. "Oh Father who is in Heaven, Hallow be your name; oh kingdom come, it will be done, on Earth as it is in Heaven; give us today bread, and forgive us for our trespassing, and we forgive those who trespassed on us; lead us into temptation and deliver us from evil; and give us power and glory forever! Thank you, Daddy. Amen."

Then Otto slept.

Chapter 22

Tom Davis:

I arrived at the station Tuesday morning eager to get to work. Things had progressed slowly so far, but I had a good feeling about the day ahead. I went over my notes. Unfortunately, while in the middle of this, I got sidetracked by other business. Terry Mulligan came storming in, complaining about some kids egging his car. I filled out a report and told him I would look into, but spent most of the time trying to calm him down. I sent Paul with him to check it out and returned to my notes.

After looking them over, I called one of the officers off patrol so someone would be at the station and then I returned to the fairgrounds. As I was getting out of my car, I heard Brian's voice. He asked me what I knew about Otto Radowski's past. I had a hunch he was asking about the story of Radowski touching a young boy, but didn't want to come out and say this in case I was wrong. I didn't want him reporting what appeared to be a nothing story.

"Anything in particular you want to know?" I asked.

"Sex pervert allegations."

It was just what I feared. I explained to him that there was nothing to the story. I told him that the boy who made the allegation was a known liar. Stockton seemed satisfied with this explanation. He left and I went to work. I first wanted to check the perimeter of the fairgrounds. I had done this before heading back to the station the night of the murder and, because I was rushed, had two of my officers make the walk around the perimeter the next morning, but now that I had more time I wanted to personally go over the ground again, hoping to see something that we might have previously missed. I walked along the entire lot along the outside of the fence but there was nothing.

Then I reentered the fairgrounds and went to the carnies' living quarters. I walked around the outside of the victim's trailer then followed the most direct path from her trailer to every trailer in the backyard, one by one. I finished by walking from her door to Radowski's. I arrived at his door and stopped. That was it. Not one shred of evidence.

I stood for a moment with my hands on my hips, trying to figure out what to do next. I decided to speak to a few of the carnies. The more I could learn about the night in question the better.

As soon as I turned around, I heard someone call out, "Chief."

It was Bill Harris. "Yes, Bill?" I said as I walked towards him.

"Um…I been thinkin'. You know I can't keep everyone here ferever."

"Yes, I know, and I appreciate you staying and how cooperative you and everybody that works for you has been."

"The thing is we gots to leave."

"What?" I asked. I was stunned and disappointed with his decision.

"Not now, but in a few days. Can't keep 'em here all winter."

"But, Bill, you want the killer caught, don't you?"

"Yes, o' course."

"Then I need more time." I explained. "Things are not unfolding as fast as I had hoped."

"Try puttin' the foot on the other shoe. What would you do if you were me?"

What did he just say? I couldn't speak for a moment. I had to compose myself.

When I put his twisted idiom out of my mind, I said, "Just give me a little more time. I promise if no progress is being made soon, I'll let you go."

He was set to argue. "Well—"

"I'd hate to have to get a court order forcing you to stay."

"All right. Do what you need."

"Thank you."

"Bye." I left him and started walking toward Shawn Keyhoe's trailer. A moment later, Bill ran back up to me and asked if I was going to town. "Not now," I told him. "I have work to do here."

"Oh," he said in a down voice and slowly walked off with his head down.

I shrugged my shoulders and moved on. I spoke to Shawn first because he had seen the victim with Radowski, and that was her only sighting with anyone just before the murder. He was sitting on the step in front of his door reading a book. "Mr. Keyhoe."

"Yes?" He looked up and closed his book. "How may I help you?"

"I'd like to ask you again about the murder night."

"Yes, sir. What would you like to know?"

"You told me you saw the victim in the backyard after closing time. Can you tell me again how that happened and what you saw?"

"Yes, certainly. I had just closed up and was coming in for the night. In the backyard, I passed Mary. She was walking with Otto Radowski."

"Did you see anything else? Did you notice if they were talking or where they were going?"

"No. I only saw them for a second. Once I passed

them that was it, that's the last I saw of them."

"Got it, thank you."

"You're welcome. Call on me for anything you need."

Next, I spoke to the girls who had seen Gino Guglielmo angry, and those who thought Mary might have had a sexual past with Bill, but learned nothing new of importance.

I left the fairgrounds extremely frustrated.

When I arrived back at the station, the first thing I did was call the county sheriff. I demanded more help. He told me he was limited in what he could offer me because of budget constraints then asked what the problem was. I explained to him that the minimal work the county detective had done was not enough.

At this, he became angry. "Tom," he said in a stern voice, "what can he do that you can't?"

"He has more experience in these—"

He cut me off. "To hell with experience. You've investigated crimes. Anything Perry can do you can. If you don't have the confidence in your own abilities, maybe you shouldn't have your job."

"I have confidence." I realized how pathetic that sounded as soon as I said it.

"Good. If the evidence leads somewhere, follow it. And if it doesn't…well, I don't need to tell you how many crimes go unsolved. And with a one-time, seemingly random crime like this, the odds of solving it are very low. If it's going to be solved, it's up to you. I can't waste any more resources to go after the killer of some carnival whore when it's unlikely to be solved anyway. Do you understand?"

"Yes, sir." I felt defeated.

"Good. We're done then," he said and hung up.

I tried to return to my notes, but wasn't very productive the rest of the day. A feeling of hopelessness kept me from concentrating like I needed to. Since I wasn't making any progress, I took care of some office business and went home early. I took off my uniform and put on something more comfortable. I ate dinner then went out.

Those first few days after the murder—that early period of the murder investigation—took a hard toll on me. It wore me down mentally. I couldn't get the victim out of my mind. I wanted to do right by her, but I had nothing: no good leads, no evidence at the scene, nothing. I had no help from the county. I didn't even have a good hunch. It was extremely frustrating. No matter how much I thought about it, I came away empty. This appeared to be the perfect crime. Not a clue was left behind. Not a clue I was able to find, anyway. I questioned whether this was my fault. Was I missing something? My confidence in my abilities as a detective was low. I knew I would not accomplish anything if I remained in this mental state. I needed to get away for the night and clear my mind.

I drove down the near empty road leading out of town. I passed the gas station on the outskirts of town where earlier I had put in $2.75 worth of gas. I put the case out of my mind and felt relieved as I pulled out of the gas station and headed down the dark road. The next lights I would see would mean I was somewhere different.

Each town I drove through was bigger than the last as I drove closer and closer to the city center. I had left the small-town for the big city lights. I drove to an area a little east of the center of downtown Cleveland. There, I stopped at a familiar bar and found a friend in a bottle. Maybe tomorrow I'd have a fresh perspective, I thought. Maybe I'd have some idea, anything, but it didn't matter now.

I hated to leave town with all of the tension in the air, but I needed to clear my head, and I couldn't escape there, not like this. Not in my blonde wig; white skirt; soft, lacy panties; and oh-so-cute pink blouse. I had done my nails and makeup and I felt beautiful. I suppose I should have shaved and gotten rid of the stubble from a long day, but I didn't care. I felt gorgeous. This was the escape I needed. It brought out my delicate, feminine side. I wasn't with a woman that night, but feeling like one brought me closer to that sex and made me feel like I wasn't alone. The soft clothes against my body were so relaxing and the panties holding me snug were mildly arousing. This was the escape I needed. It was a state of bliss.

I left the police work behind me. Tomorrow I'd go

back to being the chief of police, but for tonight I was simply Shirley.

Chapter 23

Bill Harris,
Wednesday, November 4, 1953:

As I sat down to have my mornin' coffee I wanted to think 'bout wha' to do that day to keep myself busy, but was soon sidetracked by memories o' Mary. It hit me how much I missed her. She was a good woman an' friend, an' she put on a hell o' a show. I remembered her first year werkin' fer me. She asked me 'bout ideas fer a stage name an' I suggested she could use her own name, maybe call herself "Virgin Mary." I was half jokin' but she ran with it. I laughed as I thought back to this. We got shut down pretty quick. In retrospect, it was a bad idea. The things she did with that crucifix.

What did we expect would happen in those tiny,

God-fearin' towns? It was a good memory. Lookin' back on it was the firs' time since the murder that I thought 'bout Mary an' smiled.

I finished my coffee an' still had to face the problem o' wha' to do with myself as I was stuck here fer another day. The night before I borrowed a book from Erik. I ain't never been much o' a reader 'spec fer newspaper headlines, but was so bored here figured I'd try anythin'. He lent me a collection o' Edgar Allan Poe stories in a book called *The Centenary Poe*. I tried sittin' down with it the previous night but just couldn' git into the idea o' readin'. When I woke up in the mornin' an' still had nothin' to do I figured what the hell an' sat down with the book.

The problem was that Poe wrote in that old English an' I couldn' understan' a Goddamn word. I wondered why Erik didn' give me a translated version. I got dressed an' walked over to his trailer but he wasn' there. I soon foun' him just off the midway sittin' with Pete.

"Hey, Erik, what's with the book you gave me?"

"Don't like it?"

"Do you have a translated version?"

"Translated?" he asked. "It's in English."

"Yeah," I said. "That fuckin' old English."

That little shit rolled his eyes at me. "It's in normal English," he claimed. "There are no translations."

"Fine, I'll give it another try," I said an' walked off.

I returned to my desk, sat down, an' opened the book

again. I thought fer a moment. "The Raven." That's a popular story. Even remember some movie with Lugosi 'bout it years ago. I decided to start there. I opened to "The Raven." I couldn' believe it. If this wasn' old English I didn' know what was. Who could read this shit? "Once upon a midnight dreary…" What the fuck does that mean? I read a few more lines an' they didn' make any more sense. Since I had nothin' better to do, I took this as a challenge. I pulled out my dictionary, a pencil an' paper, an' set to translate it. It would keep me busy an' maybe there was some money to be made makin' it readable.

I werked fer a long while until I finally made a little progress.

> *It was midnight and I was thinking.*
> *(unable to translate next line)*
> *I almost fell asleep when suddenly I heard tapping.*
> *It sounded like something quietly knocking at my door.*
> *"Is someone there?" I asked. "Is someone knocking at my door?"*
> *"Is that all it is and nothing else?"*

There, much better. Ah, fuck it. This took too long an' was too frustratin'. This was worse than being bored. An' who cared anyway. It's a story 'bout a goddamn talkin' bird. Who would write such a childish thing? No wonder Poe died in Bellevue. I needed a walk.

I grabbed the book an' stepped outside. I walked toward where I saw Erik an' Pete earlier so I could return the book but, from a distance, I saw that they were talkin' to that damn reporter. I wondered if Erik was tryin' to buy his soul. Anyway, I figured I'd return the book later so I returned an' put it on my desk. Then I sat down, ate a donut, an' jerked off. After that I took a walk o' the fairgrounds.

Later, when I was headin' back to my trailer, I saw Otto. He had his arms out in the air an' appeared to be talkin' to himself as he walked out beyon' the backyard. I followed from a distance.

He jus' wen' to the middle o' an empty field an' walked in circles, lookin' up, arms stretched out, like the baby Jesus. Then he looked down, still walkin' in the circles. Then looked up. Then down again. What a nut. I went back, locked myself up inside, an' had more coffee. Goddamn, it was time to git to Florida.

Chapter 24

Brian Stockton:

Wednesday I followed my daily routine. I got out of bed, put on a robe—since I sleep naked—and went to grab the papers off the front step. There I got another kick in the nuts. Despite being a slow news day, my story wasn't even the feature in the local paper, and didn't make it in any form in the Cleveland paper. Another Cleveland paper had an update on the case written by another reporter, but this was only a few lines to say nothing was new. I knew Davis was doing his best to solve this case, but I fucking wished he'd do it quicker. At this rate, no one was going to care about the story by the time he arrested anyone.

After just standing around for a few minutes, thinking, and just being pissed off, I realized I wouldn't accomplish anything standing on my front step, so I went inside, slammed the door shut, and got dressed. I needed to check with the chief to see if there was any news then split time between his office and the fairgrounds while I waited for something to break.

I went to the station.

Chief Davis looked up from his desk when I entered. "Oh, it's you."

"Anything new with the investigation?" I asked as I opened my notepad.

"Nothing to report."

"Come on, Tom, there must be something."

"I'm telling you I have nothing to report."

"This is the fourth day now. I'm beginning to think you have no chance of catching the murderer."

"Don't report that." He shook his head. He didn't look happy.

"Then it's true, you really don't have any good leads?"

He stared. It was difficult to believe that he might really have nothing.

"I thought you were just playing games—hiding something from me."

"I have leads, just nothing concrete."

"What do you have?"

"I can't tell you that."

"Who do you suspect?"

"Can't tell you. It will harm the case having it in the papers."

"Bullshit. What are you hiding from me?"

Davis stood up. "Can I level with you, off the record?"

I closed up my notepad. "Sure, off the record." I was glad to hear anything, even if I couldn't use it, just so I knew where things stood.

"I have some theories, but they are mostly hunches, most-likely scenarios. The thing is, for us to catch who did this, we need the murderer to slip up."

That didn't sound positive. "Okay," I responded.

"There wasn't any evidence at the crime scene. Nothing. The scene was perfectly clean. The killer didn't leave one trace of evidence showing they were actually there."

"Suicide?" I asked.

"Not likely. Besides a knife in the neck being an odd way to kill yourself, it was a quick, clean cut. There are generally hesitation cuts when it's a suicide. Also, the position of her body, and location of her hands, and the fact that she was naked, show she was engaged in, or preparing to engage in intercourse."

"She was being fucked when she was killed?"

"Or waiting to be. We didn't find any semen. From how she was positioned, it appears she was bent over and ready for sex when the killer reached around and stuck the knife in her neck."

"Was she forced into that position?"

"Don't know. There are no signs of force, but she could have been forced into it at knife point. It's a horrible way to go."

"That it is. How would reporting this hurt the case?"

"The lack of any other evidence. The killer didn't leave anything behind. It was as if a ghost had committed the murder. Something supernatural. If we do find the person, I don't know how we could link them to the crime. The best bet is to bluff, say we have evidence, and hope for a confession."

"I see. All right, all right. I understand," I told him.

"Thank you."

I smiled. "I'll still be checking in in case anything changes."

"I know you will."

I walked out. This was not good news for me, or for justice. Well, perhaps I would find something, or I could just report "Murder Committed by Ghost." That would go over well. I headed to the fairgrounds.

During the short drive over, I lit a cigarette and my mind drifted to the fields where this fine Turkish tobacco I was smoking grew. What a peaceful, pleasant smelling place it must be. All the hard work on this story made me think about how nice it would be just to take a break and lie naked in one of those tobacco fields. This image was fixed firmly in my mind when I suddenly realized that the fairgrounds entrance was fewer than one hundred feet away. I slowed down and turned into the parking lot. After I stopped the car, I just sat and thought back on my ride. I couldn't remember driving to the fairgrounds. I only had a memory of the tobacco field. I'll admit the complete lack of memory of a drive I had just completed scared me. I hoped I drove safely enough and did not put my life—or the life of anyone else—in danger. On some level, I must have been conscious of what I was doing or I wouldn't have made it here, but I did not know how I could have been conscious and have no memory of the drive. I opened my door and stepped out of the car. Then I lit up another cigarette to calm my nerves. I stood there smoking it until it was finished.

I entered and looked down the empty midway. Toward the intersection, I saw Arianna and another girl, so I headed in their direction. Arianna saw me, left her friend, and began walking toward me. This was a good sign. Here I had felt bad every time I flirted. I felt like it was inappropriate and unwanted, but then I'd talk to her and couldn't help myself. Well, there she was, coming in my direction, so maybe it wasn't unwanted.

"Hey," I said to her.

"Hi."

"How are you holding up?"

She shrugged her shoulders. "Fine, considering."

"Yeah, I'm sure it's tough." Then I drew a blank on what to say next. "So—" I paused as I thought. She must have thought I was an idiot with the way I stumbled for words. "Uh…" And I realized I should ask her what she's been doing around here. Maybe it would open up a casual way to ask her out. "What have you been doing to keep yourself busy?"

"Just talking to friends, a little reading. Not too much to do. Everyone serves as a reminder."

Then I dropped the hint. "Need to get you away from here."

"Yes, that would be nice," she said, but I froze.

I suddenly had major second thoughts about what I was doing—hitting on a girl who just lost her friend to a murder. Finally I said, "Well, I better get back to work."

"Yeah, of course," she said. She looked like she might have wanted me to ask her out, but it was too late.

"See you around," I said, full of regret.

As I walked away, I heard her say "Bye."

Fuck it. I couldn't let myself obsess about the ball I just dropped. I had no idea if I made the right decision, but regret wasn't going to help. Next time perhaps I'd take the chance, I thought, but for now I needed to move on and focus. I was here to mingle with the carnies and maybe learn more that I could use in my story.

I spoke to a ride operator. The conversation was neither productive nor interesting. I then approached two carnies who were sitting in lawn chairs and trying to throw rocks into a garbage can about twelve feet away. They were not good shots.

One of the men, a scrawny dirty little fellow, looked up at me. "What's up?"

Now they were both looking.

"Hi," I held out my hand and got a seemingly reluctant shake from the other guy, who was strange, almost sinister looking. "I'm Brian. I'm a reporter for the local paper."

This sinister-looking man said nothing. The scrawny guy was looking at me. "I know nothing about that murder," he declared. "I was smoking some weeds with Erik here and another guy. We didn't hear about it 'til after the fuzz came."

"That's fine. I'm not here to learn about the murder," I explained. "Just talking to people—trying to get the feel of the place and people here."

"Have a seat if you like," said the scrawny guy. "Don't think you'll learn much."

I saw an empty chair about ten feet behind them so I went over and grabbed it. The sinister-looking man had yet to say a word but had stared at me the entire time. There was something creepy about him and the way his eyes locked onto me. His goatee was devil-like. His dark hair, dark eyes, and hard features added to his evil look. I suppose I was being too difficult on him. After all, he hadn't even said anything yet. I sat down. "What do you guys do here?" I asked.

"I'm the ticket taker at the gate," the little guy said.

"Oh, yes, now I know why you look so familiar." I turned to the silent one, who the scrawny guy had called Erik. "And you?"

"The geek. I eat things."

"A carnival classic," I said.

"It's easy. Gotta eat."

"Yes, I suppose that's true." Even though I already thought he was strange, I wasn't expecting what he said next.

"How's your soul?"

"My soul?" I responded. "What do you mean?"

"There's nothing wrong with it, right? You still have it?"

I must have looked confused because the scrawny guy piped in. "Don't mind Erik, he's always trying to get souls to add to his collection."

"His collection?" I asked.

"I have twelve, not including my own," Erik said. "It's a hobby. I figure they got to be worth something in the next life. That is, if Satan doesn't make me an offer for them first."

"How do you collect?" I asked.

"People just sign them over to me. Interested?"

"In giving you my soul?"

"I'd pay you. I deal fair."

I was suddenly intrigued. My hunch was that souls didn't exist and, if they did, I doubted they could be transferred by simply signing them over. "How much?" I asked.

"A dollar?"

"For my soul? You can do better." I knew he'd go higher.

"How about five?"

"Twenty."

"I can do ten. That's all I got right now."

"Deal," I told him.

At that, this strange man gave what must have been for him a smile.

"Great," he said. "I'll go get the contract." As soon as he said that, he walked away.

"He has contracts?" I asked his friend.

"He's had them professionally drawn up."

"He takes this seriously, doesn't he?"

"You better believe it. You know you're going to have to sign it in blood, right?"

"That hadn't occurred to me. Aw, what the hell? It's ten dollars." Erik returned with the contract and a clipboard to write on. He handed it to me, with a pen.

"You can fill your name in up top with the fountain pen," then he handed me a dip pen and pin, "but the signature has to be in blood." I filled in my name and read the contract.

> *I, Brian Stockton, do transfer my eternal soul to the bearer of this document, Erik Blasko, on this, the fourth day of November, 1953.*

I shrugged my shoulders and pricked the tip of my

left index finger with the pin. A pool of blood began forming and I dipped the end of the dip pen in it then signed my name. I placed the dip pen, pin, and fountain pen on the clipboard and handed it to Erik. "Here you go."

He handed me a ten-dollar bill. "Good doing business with you."

"And with you," I said.

He walked off.

"He's going to put it in his safe," his friend told me.

"His safe?"

"I told you he is very serious about this."

"He must be. Guess I should be glad he'll take good care of my soul." I stood up. "It was nice to meet you.

"Same."

I walked away. I was hungry so I felt it was time to go spend part of my recent earnings. My only regret as I left was that I still hadn't met the World's Ugliest Man. I had to find out if that ear was real.

After grabbing a burger at the diner, I thought I would go by the police station then back to the fairgrounds. Well, that was the plan anyway. After finding out from the deputy that there was nothing new to report, I felt a little down about the story and started feeling sorry for myself. I didn't feel like hanging around the fairgrounds again quite yet. Finally, I decided to take a drive to clear my head. I wanted to forget about the story for a while, but it consumed me. I wondered who the murderer could be. I returned to my initial hunch. Was it Bill? I was still suspicious of him. I thought perhaps I should return that night and offer him a drink—or seven—to loosen him up. Maybe he would say something he shouldn't. But then I'd have to spend the evening with him. Even if he confessed to it all, was that worth spending an evening with him? Suddenly I forgot all about Bill. What appeared to be a midget riding a motorcycle passed me. He was dressed in all red, white, and blue. He looked like a fucking flag. He was like a political advertisement on wheels. Like some stunt for a small-town mayor. Out to get the midget vote. Or maybe he was a candidate himself? Would people vote for a midget? I didn't see why not, but people did lots of things I couldn't explain for reasons only they understood. I'm sure there would be some anti-midget prejudice if one was running for an office of any importance. I could see his opponent's ads against him now: "Small body equals small head. Small head equals small brain. Vote for me, my brain is normal," or some such shit. It would be an entertaining campaign, that's for sure.

Shit, I suddenly realized I had no idea where I was. I quickly dropped my "midget for mayor" thoughts and looked around. I didn't recognize a thing. I vaguely remembered taking a turn or two as I drove, but couldn't remember where or in which direction I turned. I drove on, hoping to spot some sign or marker or anything to identify my location. What I saw next wasn't a good sign.

It was an Amish family in a goddamn buggy. I was lost. I spent the rest of the day trying to find my way back to town.

Chief Davis was at the station when I arrived back there that evening. I learned from him that I had not missed anything.

I followed that with a stop at a local bar. I wasn't there to get drunk. I couldn't do that while there was still the chance of this story becoming an opportunity for me, even if that opportunity seemed to be fading. I just went to have one drink and relax a little in the atmosphere. It was a small, dark place made of some type of dark wood, and had the look of a place that hadn't changed much since the 1880s. It was a good place to wind down for the night.

Chapter 25

Arianna Lewis:

It was a lonesome week. I felt distant from everyone—everyone except Tina. She just made me feel sad. She was breaking down and really needed me. I did not know what would become of her all by herself. She really needed to pull herself together. I went to see her in the morning and was glad to hear she did okay during her night alone. The worst of it, she said, was falling asleep, which took her a few hours. It was a start, and would likely get easier and easier for her with each passing night. My thoughts turned to the scare I had the previous night. I asked Tina if Gino had checked on her last night. If he did, she did not notice. I left her to go speak with the other girls. They all had the same answer. Either they just did not notice him or, for some reason, he only came to my trailer. It really hurt me when I realized what I was doing. I was suspicious, just like my friends. I immediately felt horrible, even though I couldn't just ignore the possible danger. I walked around the fairgrounds trying to forget this.

While some of my coworkers were keeping to themselves, there were always a few out, talking. Most of the food and game stands were closed up and some of the tents had been taken down, but attractions like the funhouse and merry-go-round stood as if they were ready for business. They served as gathering places for all of us. I was glad Bill decided to let them stand until we received word we could leave. It was nice having familiar things around. They made the place less depressing. Still, I wanted to leave. We all did.

As I was casually speaking with Amy, I saw Brian—in the distance—coming in my direction. I told Amy I would speak with her later and walked to meet Brian.

"Hey," he said as we met.

It felt good seeing him. "Hi."

"How are you holding up?"

I shrugged my shoulders. "Fine, considering."

"Yeah, I'm sure it's tough. So—" he said then paused. It was cute how he was acting and trying so hard not to say the wrong thing. He asked what I had been doing to keep myself busy. When he said, "Need to get you away from here," I was sure he meant us doing something together.

"Yes, that would be nice," I said in response, expecting and hoping for an invitation to do something to follow, but I was to be disappointed.

After a long, awkward silence, he finally spoke. "Well, I better get back to work."

We said our goodbyes and he walked off.

That conversation just made me feel worse. Here, in all this hell, was this cute, nice guy, who I thought had been flirting with me and, at that moment, I thought he wanted to spend more time with me. But after he left, I felt as though I had misread him and beat myself up over it. I went and sat on one of the merry-go-round horses and teared up a little. Now I was thinking about Brian, worrying about Gino, and missing Mary. Sitting here was not helping my mood, so I wiped my eyes and wandered around again. This didn't help me feel any better. The problem was that hearing friends talking about who may have done this and fueling suspicions, which I regretted contributing to by asking about Gino, kept me feeling depressed. I soon removed myself and headed back to my trailer where I could be alone.

It was about noon and, on the way back I saw Otto having, well, an episode I suppose, for lack of a better description. I don't really know what it was. All I know is, I spotted him alone in a field, arms outstretched, looking toward the sky, and walking in circles. Then he looked down as he continued his circles, then looked back to the sky, and kept this pattern going. I'm glad Tina didn't see this. She would have flipped at the sight of this bizarre behavior. I'll admit that, under the circumstances, it made me a bit uncomfortable. This was strange, even for Otto, but we were all dealing with this in our own way.

I went to be alone. I was ready to close this chapter of my life. After thinking about it a lot, I had finally decided it was time to pursue my real dream and put this life behind me. Life was too short to spend another year stripping. Even if I wanted to spend another year on the road and with my friends, I couldn't come back here and enjoy any of it. It would never be the same.

Chapter 26

Tom Davis:

I arrived at the station early Wednesday morning. I was having my coffee when Paul arrived for duty. My initial instructions to him after the murder were to ignore it, act as chief, and take care of business as usual. Of course he—as well as the other officers under me—was briefed about the case, but I didn't want him taking an active part in the investigation. With me devoting all of my time to this, we needed someone handling my usual role. He had been a good sport about it, even though he was dying to be included. Now I needed him to follow up on a long shot lead that I didn't have time for. It was time to bring him in on the case. I knew if I gave him the chance, he would become hyperactive and start telling me all of his theories about the murder and action ideas before I had a chance to explain to him what I wanted, so I asked him to sit and not say a word. This didn't last long. I began with, "I want to talk to you about the murder."

"I've been thinking about that and I have an idea as to how to—"

"Paul." I held my hand up and stopped his hundred-mile-an-hour talking. "Listen." He stayed quiet. "I had a conversation with Gino Guglielmo. He runs the girly show. He told me that on the first night of the carnival the victim had some trouble with a patron. Guglielmo called it a tussle. He said the guy was hitting on her and he kicked him out. We need to find this man. I know it is a long shot, but it is possible that this mystery man was angry and tried to exact revenge, or that he came back for another play at her, and she refused."

"I see."

"The problem is that we have no lead on who this man is, and Guglielmo's description of him leaves much to be desired. I'll get it copied for you, but it won't help."

His body stiffened with anticipation. "Help me with what?"

"I need you to start patrolling the town on foot. While doing this, I want you to ask any man you come in contact with if he attended any of the girl shows and, for those who did, ask if they saw the man who harassed her and if they can identify him. Of course you have to do this discreetly."

"Yes, Tom."

"Hopefully, the guy we're looking for is a local man, otherwise we'll never find him." I chose Paul for this role instead of someone else in the department because of his higher rank and time on the force. I thought people might share more with him than anyone else I could send. I did worry, however, that he would be too enthusiastic.

"I will crack the case," Paul vowed. He was visibly excited by the assignment, as shown by his enthusiasm and the smile he could not hide.

"Remember, it is very important to use discretion when making inquiries."

"Yes, of course," he said.

I didn't want him to get too eager, as he had a habit of doing. If the man we were after was the killer, I preferred he didn't know we were looking for him. The possibility that Paul would stop and question this man, however, was a risk we had to take.

"That will be all," I told him. "Why don't you go out on patrol now?"

"I'm on it, Chief." He held his head high and proudly walked off.

After Paul left, I sat at my desk to look over my interview and crime scene notes, hoping to see something I didn't yet see. While I was doing this, that goddamned reporter came in. He just added to my already growing frustration.

After I acknowledged his presence, he asked if I had

anything new to report. I told him I didn't but he kept pushing me until he hit right on my fear.

"This is the fourth day now," he said. "I'm beginning to think you have no chance of catching the murderer."

"Don't report that," I said and shook my head.

"Then it's true, you really don't have any good leads? I thought you were just playing games—hiding something from me."

"I have leads, just nothing concrete," I said.

This was true. I had theories, just no evidence to back them up. This didn't stop his questions. Finally, I stood up. I could tell he wasn't going to let this go so I thought I'd try being honest with him, then maybe he would stop with these distracting interruptions. Besides, this would give me a chance to vent a little about the lack of evidence. "Can I level with you, off the record?"

He put away his notepad. "Sure, off the record," he said.

I explained how little evidence there was and let him know what I did know. I did not get into suspects. I didn't need him following someone around because I suspected them. When I finished explaining what little I knew from the crime scene, he asked, "How would reporting this hurt the case?"

"The lack of any other evidence. The killer didn't leave anything behind. It was as if a ghost had committed the murder. Something supernatural. If we do find the person, I don't know how we could link them to the crime. The best bet is to bluff, say we have evidence, and hope for a confession."

Maybe I shouldn't have told him this, but, despite what I thought of him, I knew he would do the right thing and not report it. And it felt good to vent.

He seemed satisfied with my explanation and left. I turned my attention back to my notes.

Chapter 27

Otto Radowski:

Old Otto couldn't take it no more. Too much on my mind. Too much pain and worry. Thinking about Mary—about the horrible thing that happened to her. Thinking about my friends and what they think of me. It make Otto hurt deep down. Had feeling in my heart that wouldn't go away. A pain—a strong pain. Couldn't take it no more. I had a little meltdown, I did. I walked outside, about noon, oblivious to everyone and everything.

I just wandered around for a while—wandering until I reached an open area of the fairgrounds. What was I to do? Oh poor Mary. I just walked, thinking, walking in small circles, arms stretched out, alternately looking down at the ground while I walked a few circles and up to the sky while I walk more. Over and over. So sad. Otto so very sad. I walked, and thought, and let out my pain, circle after circle after circle.

Otto walked in circles looking down. Otto walked in circles looking up. Over and over again. It helped old Otto think. Nowhere to go. Couldn't get lost if I just kept up the circles. Just walking and thinking and trying to release some of the pain from my heart. Otto keep walking in those circles, looking up for a while—looking down for a while. I did this. I did it, and did it, and did it, and did it. Walking and thinking. Trying to straighten out my head and just being sad. Just kept walking in circles. Thirty-six times I did. Looking up, then down, and going in circles thirty-six times. Then Otto dropped to my knees and cried. Oh how sad. Poor Mary. And me going through accusations and all. So sad. So very sad.

I cried for a good while—let it out, let it all out. Flow pain, flow out of old Otto. Go. Please go out. Tears flowed, pain flowed, out. Out! Oh, hurts. Crying helped it all out but still hurt. Continued crying for long time. I was on my knees on the ground crying, Otto was.

When I recovered, I got enough of the grief out to think correctly and I realized how out of control I was. The pain and hurt had taken over. What just happened wasn't me, no. It was pain. Now with my head clear, I decided it was probably best for me to be alone for a while. I returned to my trailer to stay until this all over. Otto so sad. So very sad.

Chapter 28

Bill Harris,
Thursday, November 5, 1953:

It was another fuckin' day stuck here. I was havin' some coffee to gits me goin'. Fer somethin' different, instead o' black, I put a little cinnamon in the coffee this mornin'. My old buddy Eunuch Al turned me on to that.

As soon as I sat down, the copper knocked. He just wanted to talk 'bout my werkers. He told me I could git dressed an' he'd meet me outside.

We walked 'round an' talked 'bout some o' the people here. He questioned me again 'bout Otto's past.

"Have you remembered anything else you might have heard about Radowski's past?" he asked me.

"No, nothin'. He don't talk 'bout it so I don't ask."

"You didn't ask him about it when you hired him?"

"Nope. Just asked 'bout his carnival experience an' made him do Bozo fer me."

"How about Guglielmo, did the fight he had with the victim really not concern you?"

"No. He's a hothead. That kin' o' stuff happens with him."

"And he's never gotten violent?"

"No. Nothin' I ever heard 'bout. Just screams a lot."

Then we got to talkin' 'bout other stuff so much that this didn' seem like no official police interview. We spent lots o' time not even talkin' 'bout the crime. When we walked by the merry-go-roun' I just happens to mention it was made in 1894 an' we ga talkin' a good five minutes 'bout it. It is a classic an' he understood that. He seemed to have a real appreciation fer carnivals, an' carnies, an' the art that went into it all. He spent much time examinin' the merry-go-roun' an' the Devil's Lair. He was fascinated with the stuff.

As we walked away from the Devil's Lair, he asked me where the dead cowboy was. I told him McCurdy was packed an' ready to go home fer the winter. He stopped an' looked at me.

"Be honest, is he real?" the cop asked.

"Yeah, he is," I told him.

His eyes lit up. "No shit? And the story behind him, is it true?"

"That's the story he came with, an' I got an old

newspaper confirmin' his display after his death. What I knows is he's a real corpse an' what that old paper says."

"That is amazing. He's so well-preserved."

"Yep, he is. We're very careful with him so he don't break."

"Wow," he said as he shook his head. We began to walk an' then he stopped again, this time to ask, "That 'World of the Future' exhibit, how do you guys know that stuff will happen?"

The truth is that exhibit was just some bullshit I threw together from space toys an' the like. I bought most o' it at a toy store on Hollywood Boulevard when I was in Los Angeles last winter, but he seemed so childlike an' innocent at that moment that I didn' have the heart to tell him this, so I lied. "We got experts to come in an' set it up," I said. "Futuromitists. They was expensive but well worth the investment."

"They sure were," he said.

I had thought he was smart but now I wasn' so sure. As he talked, a big gust o' win' blew his hair all over an' the long hair on top covered his face.

I hadn' thought o' it as bein' long enough to cover his face 'cause o' the short hair on the side an' got a good laugh at that. Watchin' him fix his hair reminded me o' someone an' I was distracted from our talk until I figured out who.

Then I realized it was my buddy from Memphis, hunchback Sal. Jus' somethin' similar 'bout both o' 'em.

Er maybe he reminded me o' Sal's old lady. I dunno, he jus' made me think o' Sal.

We continued to walk, talkin' 'bout the carnival. He was so into it I hoped it didn' distract him from his police werk. Before he left me, he told me I had a pleasantly simple carnival, like ones he visited when he was a kid. I thought that was kin' o' a left-handed compliment but just said, "Thanks." I saw no reason to pick a fight with the law.

Chapter 29

Brian Stockton:

Thursday morning fared poorly for my story in both the Cleveland and local paper. Ike made all the headlines, locally and nationally, with comments on various state and local elections and his bashing of the Russians, who he said were setting up impossible conditions that were stalling a meeting between the Big Four Powers about Germany and Austria. There was no coverage of the murder in any of the Cleveland papers, and even in the local paper, it was just a little box stating nothing was new, which took me all of thirty seconds to write last night. If only there was a break, something else to write about, but what? I had nothing, and was unsure of where to go for answers.

As I cleaned myself up that morning, I tried looking

at the case from Chief Davis's point of view, and think about what I would do to solve it if I was sheriff. But, as I went through the list and realized he had probably done all the things I was thinking, my mind wandered to the idea of what kind of sheriff I would make. The only thing I'd probably do different with the murder is that I'd have most of my men devoting all of their time to the case. In a town like this, there was not much else to worry about. I'd cut the police force in half and stop wasting resources on teens being teens, minor speeding, harmless jaywalking on empty streets, and drugs.

I'd let people live. The problem with the police, and laws, is they intrude too much in people's lives when they are not protecting them from anyone but themselves. This made me angry. I'd speak out against this in my campaign for sheriff. I'd scream at the top of my lungs, "I will not enforce useless laws!" If I could get the youth and freaks to the polls, I could actually win this thing!

What the fuck was I saying? I wasn't running for sheriff. My pulse was up and I am sure my anger against the current system was visible in my face. I took a deep breath and, as I walked to the car, I tried to get my mind off my campaign for sheriff. I needed to calm down so I could do my job. I got in my car and headed to the police station.

Davis was at his desk in the main room when I walked in. "Good morning," I said. He looked up. "Anything new?" I asked.

"Nothing."

"Honestly? There's nothing you're holding back from me, is there?"

"Not a thing. I wish there was."

"Okay then. I'll check in later."

He nodded and I left. Since Chief Davis didn't have any news for me, I decided to drive into Cleveland and talk to the coroner who worked on the case, and some of the city detectives, to get their opinions. I hoped maybe they'd thought of something that Davis hadn't, something I could follow up on. It turned out to be a big waste of time. The coroner didn't have anything at all to add, and only one detective spoke to me. He gave the opinion that the killer was probably someone who knew her but he didn't have any evidence to base that on, or suggestions for what I should do, so I had lunch—a very good corned beef sandwich—then headed back to town.

On the drive back, I went through the list of suspects in my mind. The problem was there wasn't any real evidence to pin down anyone. I was starting to think that maybe it was the clown. I would have suspected him, even if he hadn't been accused of being a sex pervert in the past and hadn't had the victim's cat. The problem was there wasn't—from what I knew—any direct evidence against him or anyone else. The cat thing was suspicious, but it wasn't proof that he killed her. Perhaps there was a good reason she asked him to watch her cat. I couldn't think of what that reason might be, but there may have been one. Then I had a thought. Maybe the murder was completely random. Perhaps it was a doper. I knew the effects of hard drugs for reasons better left unsaid. Maybe some guy was on some drug-induced high and didn't know what he was doing? There were surely hard drug users in that carnival bunch. What the hell was I thinking? More evidence would have been left behind. It would have been sloppy. This was clean. It had to be planned.

It was about 3:45 in the afternoon when I got back into town. I checked at the station and Davis was out. His deputy Paul was there. He told me there was nothing new, so I headed down to the fairgrounds. I didn't expect to learn anything, but I had nothing else to do. I'd rather spend my time there and end up with nothing in tomorrow's edition than waste time writing about some useless local news. And anyway, my editor kept my schedule clear so I could devote as much time as needed to this story. It was the best thing that could have happened to me while working for a small-town paper, and I did not intend to miss any opportunities.

When I arrived at the fairgrounds, I found that none of the carnies were in a talkative mood. Who could blame them? Their friend had been savagely murdered, and they were stuck living here indefinitely. The tension could be felt in the air. I felt sympathy for them. My thoughts turned to Arianna. That sweet girl didn't deserve this. I went to check how she was doing.

I knocked on her door.

Arianna answered. She was alone and seemed happy to see me. "Brian," she said.

"Hey, Arianna," I said. "I wanted to see how you were doing."

"Eh," she responded.

"Yeah, sorry. Dumb question," I said. Then I got to the point of my visit. "I was thinking. I know it must be depressing here. Would you like to come to town with me? Maybe get something to eat?" I made it sound as casual as possible. My nerves calmed when my invitation was greeted with a cute smile.

"I'd love to," she told me. "Just give me a moment to freshen up."

"Sounds good," I said and, after she closed her door, I lit up some of that Turkish tobacco. I suddenly felt happy and relaxed.

After a few minutes, she emerged from her trailer. She was not too dressed up, for obvious reasons, but it didn't matter. She looked amazing. I felt proud to be with her.

During the short drive, we talked about movies. I parked on the end of the main street in town. At this time of evening, most the shops were closed but I did not think it mattered. The point was to get her away from the depressing fairgrounds and spend some time together. While walking up the street, we saw the most frightening baby. I could tell Arianna noticed him too. His father was pushing him in a stroller and the mother was with them. They weren't a bad-looking couple, but that baby, oh that baby.

After they passed, I said to Arianna in a low voice, "That baby has his parents' worst features."

"You're so cruel," she said with a giggle.

It may have been mean, but it was true. That nose, those eyes, and that scrunched up face. What a hideous baby.

We ate at a local diner. Over the course of the meal, I learned a lot about her. We discussed everything from music, to Negro rights, to our life goals. The civil rights conversation was pretty intense. It began with her mention of blues musician Josh White. I said he was a good choice, meaning a good choice of someone to listen to, then she said, "The first time I heard 'Uncle Sam Says' I cried. Very poignant."

"That should be the theme song for the Negro civil rights movement," I told her. "It captures the state of America for the colored man so clearly and simply. Like you said, it is so moving."

She nodded. "Songs like that, or anything that carries that powerful a message, could have a strong influence. It's all about finding a way to get the message out and educate people. Entertainment and art is a great way to do that."

I shook my head at her naivety.

"But you agree with the message," she said.

"But who's gonna listen? It's just talking to the converted. All the self-proclaimed nigger haters out there are not just going to agree that we are all created equal and should have the same rights, just like they didn't simply agree to end slavery almost one-hundred years ago."

"So what's your solution?"

"Violence. A revolution. Get the guns and take to the streets." I was suddenly very worked up as I explained to her why I thought violence was the answer. The fact was the ignorant were not going to simply change their opinion. To me change by force was the only way to accomplish anything. "When some leader starts that revolution, I'm there," I told her. "Small outbreaks of violence will not cut it. I want to see a well-organized, national revolution behind a charismatic leader. The only people who won't have sympathy are those already trying to oppress the Negro. And the ones who won't go along—kill 'em. We'll all be better off. There's too many stupid people anyway."

I suddenly noticed in her an uneasiness as my eyes lit up with my push for violence. While we agreed on what should happen, we strongly disagreed on how to get there. She was obviously disturbed by my rant and ready for me to stop it. I thought she was naive thinking change could happen peacefully, but that we didn't agree on how the Negro civil rights movement should unfold wasn't worth ruining the evening over, so I calmed myself and changed the subject by asking her about herself.

"What are you going to do when you leave town?"

"I think I want to go to school."

"Go to school?" I asked. "For what?"

"I want to become a veterinarian."

It took me a moment to gather my thoughts. A career like that wasn't what I expected her to say. She seemed smart from our conversations. I realized I was guilty of basing some of my judgment of her on other people. Even if they seemed smart, strippers usually were not very intelligent or educated, and certainly didn't fit the profile of a career woman. If anything, one would expect strippers who left the business by choice to want to have the things most girls want—a family.

She must have sensed my surprise, or I was just quiet for too long. "What's wrong?" she asked me. "Can't a woman have a career?"

"Of course you can," I said as I tried to arrange my thoughts. "You just..." I paused as I searched for what to say. "I wasn't expecting that. Most women just want a husband and a family. And there's your—" I stopped my-self as I realized what I was saying, but it was too late.

"My what?" she asked.

I was so worried I offended her. "Well, um, you know..." I paused and looked at her, but she was going to make me finish the sentence. "Your job."

"A stripper can't go to college?"

"It's just not normally done."

"So, you don't think I can do it?"

That question was like a slap to the face. I had been horrible. "I know you can do it," I stated and I meant it.

I had already known she was a sweet and caring girl, but I didn't know the smart and strong woman underneath. Most strippers, well, there isn't much to them. They normally have issues with men or other problems, are desperate for money, and usually not that smart. But none of this applied to her. I now saw that she really did think of her job as an opportunity to see the country and have some fun, nothing more. She wanted to go to school and become a veterinarian, and from what I saw in her, I knew she would do it.

After the meal, I asked her, "Do you want to walk through town?"

She smiled. "Yes, that should be nice."

We walked on, mostly in silence, with only a few words here and there. When we approached a business that had underneath it an old Underground Railroad site, I pointed it out just to say something. She smiled and seemed interested in this little fact. My feeling was that, even though not much was being said, she enjoyed my company like I enjoyed hers. When we came to the river, we crossed to the waterfall side of the street. We leaned on the fence over the fall and just stood there, looking and listening and not saying a word. After a little silence, I put my arm around her. She leaned into me. I don't know how long we stood there. It didn't matter. However long it was, I wished it could have lasted longer: just me, her, the sound of the water, and the beautiful night view.

As we walked back to the car, Arianna thanked me for the dinner and night out.

"Thank you for accepting. Anyway, one of your friends helped pay for it by buying my soul," I joked.

"I see you met Erik. How much you get?"

"Ten dollars."

"That's it? He gave me forty for mine."

"Forty? Oh, that hurts."

"I wouldn't worry about it. It's free money."

"I hope so," I said.

"You hope so? You don't believe in souls, do you?"

"I don't know. Why do you sound surprised?"

"Because you sold yours."

"Oh yeah, good point." She had me there. "Well," I continued, "I don't really, I just, you know, what if it does exist? Don't you ever worry that you sold yours?"

"No." She laughed. "The concept of a soul is so absurd why would I worry about it? It was obviously invented by man to make him feel better about death."

"Maybe, I don't know. I mean, if there is a God, he may be mad that I sold my soul on principle, even if it doesn't exist."

"And if there's a Santa Claus, he may not bring me presents because of my job. I don't think either of us have to worry about how these fictional beings will judge us."

She was more sure than about this than I was. I now wished I had thought of all this before I made the sale.

"How can you be so sure there is no God?" I asked.

"Reason. If you think about it, God really is a ridiculous concept, an idea obviously created out of fear of death and a need to explain the unexplainable. Fortunately, we have science for that now."

I knew what she was saying but couldn't fully agree. I had always been so unsure about these things. "Is God any crazier than any other explanation of how we came to be?"

"I think so," she stated. "An all-powerful being who has just always been and who created everything?"

I didn't know what to say. She made sense, but I was still unsure.

"Well, I hope you're right," I said. "I mean, I don't, I'd rather there be a God and Heaven and all that, I just mean about my soul, since I sold it and all."

"I know what you mean," she assured me.

"I still don't get." Then I paused, second-guessing whether to continue this conversation. I didn't want to piss her off.

She broke the momentary silence. "You still don't get what?"

"Well, you know, if you believe the Bible, and if there is a God, not believing in him is a really big sin. It can cause you to go to Hell. Isn't it, you know, safer to believe?"

"I would love there to be a God and an afterlife, but how do you make yourself believe in something that you don't?" She made a good point. "Besides, me just deciding to believe it doesn't make it true," she added.

She had given me something to think about. If there was a God, I suppose he'd know how we all really feel deep down, and, if his ego is so large that he needs everyone to believe in him, I suppose Arianna putting on an insincere belief won't help her reach Heaven. I wondered how he'd take my "if" feeling toward his existence. I thought he was probably there because I couldn't think of a better explanation for everything, but I'll admit I was never one hundred percent sold on the idea.

I pushed these thoughts out of my mind. I was having too good of a night to worry about whether God was some egotistical asshole who needed to punish everyone who didn't believe in him, or didn't believe in him enough. Something like that could preoccupy me and worry me for days. But I wouldn't let it tonight. Not while I was with this pretty girl who made me feel so good inside.

We reached my Fleetline and I opened the door for her. "Thank you," she said as she sat down. I got in on the other side and started the car. As I pulled out of the parking space she said, "Thank you for taking me out. I enjoyed it."

"Thank you for accepting. You sure it wasn't too cold?"

"No, I like it. Not cold, just crisp. Beats too warm anytime. It wasn't too cold for you, was it?" she asked in a joking way.

"No, no. It was fine."

After some silence she said to me, "I understand you wanting more, but this really is a nice place—a great little town."

"Oh, it is," I agreed. "If I could do what I wanted to do here, I'd stay." I pulled into the fairgrounds parking lot. All was quiet as I drove to the gate and stopped the car. I turned to Arianna and smiled. She returned the smile.

"Arianna," I said, "There is something I have wanted to ask you."

"Ask away."

"The World's Ugliest Man, is his ear real?"

She burst out laughing, which I took as a good sign. I had worried I might offend her by asking about her freakish friends, so I had been holding this question back. "Yes," she said, still laughing. "Dennis's ear is real."

"Oh, my God," I said in disgust. I was expecting to hear it was a well-done fake. "I…" I searched for words to express what I was feeling, but came up blank. "I don't know what to say. I hadn't expected that answer. I hope I didn't offend him."

"How could you have offended him?" she asked.

"With that ear, he must be able to hear us."

"Stop," she said, laughing. "You're bad."

When the laughing stopped, I said, "I'm sorry I asked, I had wanted to kiss you, but now, with the image of that ear in my—"

At that moment she leaned in and kissed me. She even tasted sweet. It was then that a police car pulled up.

Chapter 30

Tom Davis:

It had been two more days of no progress. After an uneventful Tuesday, my night out did me good. I had come back excited and ready to go the next morning. But the following day, I made no progress and got so desperate I sent Paul out on what was probably a wild goose chase, and by Thursday morning my newfound inspiration had completely faded. I started to develop a hunch that maybe Otto Radowski was the guilty party, so I spent that morning on the phone learning more about him, but found out nothing important. Then I visited the fairgrounds.

I had a distracting talk with Bill where I found out nothing helpful to the case, but enjoyed myself greatly learning about the carnival.

We were approaching the impressive merry-go-round when I said, "Your merry-go-round is beautiful. It looks very well crafted."

"Thank you," he said. "I was thrilled when I bought it from a park that had closed down. It was built in 1894."

The fact that it was an antique made it even more beautiful in my eyes. We stepped up on the platform and I examined the fine craftsmanship as he told me about this historic attraction.

Next, we walked up to the spooky house. "It's another work of art, just like the merry-go-round," I told him.

"You want to go in?"

"Really, now?"

"Sure, why not. It won't be runnin', but you can see everythin'."

I couldn't believe this great opportunity. I was so excited. The spooky house was always a favorite of mine, and this one was special. I had seen it when the carnival was open, but that doesn't compare to a private tour like this where I could walk through the spooky house instead of riding through in the little car. I tried to temper my excitement and we entered. He unlocked it, let us in, and then turned on some lights.

"Take your time," he told me.

I slowly entered. The lights were few so the place was dark. As I was enjoying this artistic creation, I realized I needed to take my time for another reason. I had not checked this out on the night of the murder. I should never have skipped it. Thinking back, I remembered that I had been in such a hurry to see as much as possible, as quickly as possible, that I skipped some of the larger attractions that would have taken too much time to explore. I did send two officers out the following day, and they examined the Devil's Lair and other exhibits, but they were not trained detectives, so I didn't expect them to have noticed anything but obvious clues. Not looking this over myself was a bad mistake. What if the murderer had made his escape to here? It was doubtful, but there could be evidence. I needed to look at everything. I went slow. There were three sections, the cemetery, the dead—coffins, skeletons, that kind of stuff that would be in the cemetery ground—and Hell. As I turned the corner, we left the cemetery and came upon a large wooden coffin. I touched it. It was a quality piece.

"Is it okay if I open this?" I asked Bill.

"Go ahead."

I slid my fingers inside the door and slowly pulled. There was a slight resistance. When I had it open more, I could see why. There was a metal rod attached to the inside of the door.

"What does this do?" I asked.

"Opens an' closes the door."

I remembered the rattling door from my ride through the spooky house. I glanced back inside, saw nothing, closed the door, and continued. Walking through the closed, turned off spooky house, was a major thrill for me. And I must add that it being turned off, along with the event that had me here, made it even spookier then it normally would have been. As we entered Hell, it was as if I could feel evil in here. I hesitantly walked up to the devil. I knew it wasn't real, but the circumstances and the sight of the devil in this dimly lit room had gotten to me. Nothing had been said between Bill and me since we had entered Hell. It was an eerie silence but I didn't know how to break it, so I stayed quiet as I examined Satan. He was a handcrafted wooden piece with beautiful detail. Staring at his evil red face gave me chills.

After a moment of just taking it all in, I stepped back and continued, toward the exit. "Scary place you have here."

"It does the job."

We left the spooky house and continued our walk. As we walked by an empty spot, I thought for a moment then remembered that's where the supposed dead cowboy had been. "Where's the dead cowboy?" I asked him.

"McCurdy is packed away fer the trip home an' the winter."

"Be honest, is he real," I asked.

To my shock and surprise, he nodded. "Yeah, he is."

His answer gave me goose bumps. "No shit?" I responded. I wanted so badly to ask him to see it again, but it was already packed away and didn't want to put Bill through the trouble. I did ask, "And the story behind him, is it true?"

"That's the story he came with, an' I got an old newspaper confirmin' his display after his death. What I knows is he's a real corpse an' what that old paper says."

"That is amazing. He's so well preserved."

"Yep, he is. We're very careful with him so he don't break."

"Wow," was all I could say. This was too much for words. I felt a childlike excitement. We took a few more steps and I stopped again. We were in front of the "World of the Future" exhibit and I had to ask him about it. "That 'World of the Future' exhibit, how do you guys know that stuff will happen?"

"We got experts to come in an' set it up. Futuro-mitists. They was expensive but well worth the invest-ment."

"They sure were," I told him.

They really were. It was a very professional, detailed exhibit, so I wasn't surprised that experts put it together. It was memorable and educational. I could have spent the rest of the day talking about this stuff, but I had work to do. I moved on from Bill and talked to some others about the carnival. I'll admit that I really enjoyed this. I had al-ways loved carnivals so this was a real treat. Having worked at a carnival in the past didn't change that. But enjoyment wasn't why I was socializing. I hoped by en-gaging in some casual conversation in an informal setting that maybe anyone hiding anything would slip up, but this did not happen.

I left the fairgrounds, feeling as lost as ever.

I struggled with what to do. I couldn't keep these people in town forever. If I didn't get a break soon, I'd have to let them go, most likely letting the murderer go free as well. It was a depressing thought but a possibility that I needed to face. Maybe detective Perry was right. Maybe this would go unsolved. This weighed heavily on my mind as I drove into town.

I needed to break this feeling of helplessness before I could have any hope of being productive when going over the case yet again, so I stopped at the diner in town, brought my newspaper in, ate, and read to clear my mind. I was still down when I left.

When I returned to the station, I found it empty. Paul must have still been out on patrol. Normally I'd be upset that he didn't leave someone here, but tonight this was good. I needed the quiet time to think. I grabbed a cup of water and sat at my desk to reevaluate the entire case. I hoped I would find something I had previously missed. I went through suspect by suspect.

Was it Otto Radowski? Based on what I knew, I couldn't just dismiss him. There was no direct evidence linking him to the crime, but there were questions, like why did Radowski have the victim's cat? That was strange. He was seen with the victim shortly before her death and he had no alibi. But what was the motive? Unrequited love? There was no strong evidence to support that. Was he just crazy and finally snapped, just choosing her because she was available? I didn't have the answers.

Was it Gino Guglielmo? Probably not, his alibi seemed airtight. He only left the show for a short time that night to find the victim and complain to Bill about her absence. But this hardly seemed like enough time to commit the crime and return with no blood on himself and leaving no evidence.

Bill Harris? He had no alibi, but again, what was the motive? Again, unrequited love, maybe? But there was no evidence to show that he was lusting after her.

Then my mind turned to that damned reporter. He suddenly had this important story to cover. He seemed to be the only one who had anything to gain from all of this. Ah, I was being crazy. I had no evidence to suggest that he was the guilty one. It was a ridiculous thought.

Was it a patron of the show? Although I had thought it was probably a carny, the possibility that it was a customer now seemed like a decent bet. It could have been someone who was fooled by her motel room key scam, became angry, and sought revenge. Maybe someone whose sexual advances were rebuffed. Possibly it was the man she had a fight with a week before. The idea became more intriguing to me as I pondered it. Maybe he was angry, returned to the show on the last night, followed her back to her trailer, sexually assaulted and murdered her. It was beginning to make some real sense. I was really starting to believe that this was the man. And if it was a carny…well, I had interviewed them all and searched everywhere. If it was one of them, they hid it well, and I probably wouldn't find any evidence against the guilty party. I was thinking this path was hopeless and that it was probably time to let the carnies leave. I felt guilty about even thinking this, like I was giving up, but what else could I do that I hadn't done? What could I find that I hadn't found? Anyway, I could still investigate the case. It would just be more difficult after they left. I couldn't keep them here forever.

Just then, Paul burst through the door yelling, "I've found him! I've found him!"

"Found who?" I asked.

"The man at the show. The one I've been looking for!"

This was great news.

"Who is it?"

"Lucas Applewhite."

"Goddamn."

Lucas Applewhite was a strange character. He lived in a small shack on the outskirts of town. He was basically a hermit who never had much contact with anyone.

"Let's go," I told my deputy and we were quickly on our way.

When we arrived at the Applewhite place, a light was on but there were no sounds from inside and no answer when we knocked at the door. The door had no lock so we let ourselves in. We were immediately hit with the strong, sickening smell of a dead body. Lucas's body was sprawled out in the middle of the room. His position and the beer bottle near him suggested he died of a heart attack or some similar sudden natural cause. A quick look at the body made it clear that he had been dead for well over a week, not that I was a doctor but that was my opinion anyway. If that was the case, and I believed that it was, then he had been dead before the murder. Still, we searched his home for any evidence we could find, but of course we found nothing, and the recent excitement over identifying Applewhite turned to despair.

Before we left, I phoned the coroner. I asked him to examine the body and told him the estimated time of death was important, but at this point, I was sure of one thing: Lucas Applewhite was not the killer.

Paul and I didn't talk as we drove back to the station. Once there, Paul was still quiet. I understood why. He was sure he had broken the case. A part of me had believed that too. It didn't matter now. I told him he should go home and get some sleep. When he left, I lit a cigarette and sat back in my chair. So it wasn't the man she had a fight with. Who then? My thoughts turned back to the carnies. Could it have been Radowski? He had been accused of some pretty bad things. I believed him when he denied the allegations, but why? Because the sheriff where it happened didn't believe the boy? Just because the kid had lied in the past did not mean he lied then. Maybe being molested by Radowski messed him up and turned him into the liar he is? Did I believe Radowski because there appeared to be no evidence? Just because we couldn't prove anything doesn't mean he was innocent. And the way he spoke and rambled on, was he just that way or was he hiding something? I shook my head in frustration. I had no answers, only questions. Just then, the phone rang.

Chapter 31

Arianna Lewis:

Tension around the fairgrounds was at its boiling point. Everyone was frightened and sick and tired of being here. We all just wanted to get away and go home. I wished to be in Kansas. For me, the others in the carnival made me feel so much worse. They were my friends. They were all supposed to be friends, but there was anger and suspicion in the air. One thing had changed, however. Earlier in the week, everyone had their own individual theories about who the murderer was, but over the last few days, many let go of their own theories. Now, most of the suspicion fell upon one person: Otto. This isn't to say that everyone was convinced he was the guilty party, just that they now all seriously considered the possibility that it might be him. I tried staying out of these conversations, so I don't know if they knew anything, but I doubt it. I think they just wanted someone to blame. Whatever it was, I didn't want to be a part of it.

I went inside to escape. I was sitting in my bed when there was a knock at my door. I opened it and was happy with who I saw. "Brian," I said.

"Hey, Arianna. I wanted to see how you were doing."

"Eh," I said. What else could I say?

"Yeah, sorry. Dumb question. I was thinking. I know it must be depressing here. Would you like to come to town with me? Maybe get something to eat?"

I instantly smiled. I was delighted. Not only did I need to go somewhere, anywhere, just to get away, but I also liked him. I sensed that he was attracted to me as well. I had doubted his interest in me yesterday, but I now thought his hesitance to ask me to do something was just nerves. We had both flirted. Still, he had work to do, so taking me out of here for a night was a nice thing to do. "I'd love to. Just give me a moment to freshen up."

"Sounds good," he said with a smile.

He looked so cute standing there. I closed the door and took a few minutes to clean myself up. I stepped outside and said, "Ready to go."

He exhaled smoke from his cigarette and smiled. "You look amazing."

I knew I didn't but after this week it was nice to hear.

"Thank you," I replied.

"This way." As we walked to his car, I suddenly felt a bit nervous. We were both silent on the way. At his car, he opened the door for me. After pulling into the street, the silence stopped. "See any good movies lately?" he asked.

"I haven't seen many all summer," I told him. "A few weeks back some of the girls and I saw *Abbott and Costello Meet Dr. Jekyll and Mr. Hyde.*"

"How was it?"

"It was just so-so. A few funny moments, but most of it fell flat. It just didn't make me laugh that much. You see anything good lately?"

"*The War of the Worlds.*"

"How was that? I've wanted to see it." He was very complimentary of the story and visuals. His only criticism was that he wished it were closer to the H. G. Wells book, which wouldn't bother me because I have never read it. "I'll have to see it," I told him.

A moment later, we pulled into town. Brian found a spot on the street right away and parked. "Charming place," I observed after getting out of the car.

"It is," he agreed. "It's a quiet place." It was a quaint looking small-town. Most of the buildings were probably built in the second half of last century. There was a gazebo in the middle of the town but, instead of a town square, the main road split into a "V" and the gazebo was in the middle of that triangle. The sides of the roads opposite this middle section were lined with businesses and shops. We had parked at one end of the street and walked from there.

Almost as soon as we started walking we passed a mother, father, and baby that the father was pushing in a stroller—a baby who looked like a little Edward G. Robinson, not a good look for a baby. Once we passed them, Brian whispered, "That baby has his parents' worst features."

"You're so cruel," I told him with a little laugh. While it was mean, he was correct.

"You hungry?" he asked.

"I am."

"There's a diner just ahead if you want to go there. Good diner type food."

"Let's do it."

We walked about a half of a block and were there. It was a weeknight so it wasn't too crowded. There were two pairs of high schoolers in the booth behind us. Football players in lettermen jackets, each with a girl. Had it not been a school night the place probably would have been overrun with teens—boys with pompadours and wearing leather jackets and girls in poodle skirts and bobby socks. We chatted about the crowd, the town, what we ordered, while we waited for our food.

Brian had a cheeseburger and I had a patty melt. We both had Coca-Cola with vanilla syrup. I could have had the same meal in any diner in any part of the country. I liked that. It felt familiar. I needed that tonight. Then "Music! Music! Music!" played on the jukebox. "Oh, I love this song," I said, and Brian gave me a look of subtle disapproval. "Let me guess, you don't like it?"

He shook his head. "I'm more into blues."

"Who says you can't like both?"

"You a blues fan?"

"Not all, but certain artists. I've recently been listening to something a little older: Josh White's Southern Exposure."

"Good choice."

"The first time I heard 'Uncle Sam Says' I cried," I admitted. "Very poignant."

In a more serious tone Brian stated, "That should be the theme song for the Negro civil rights movement. It captures the state of America for the colored man so clearly and simply. Like you said, it is so moving."

I nodded. I was glad we agreed on this issue. It's one of those issues that, if someone is on the wrong side, it will strongly sour my opinion of them. As we continued on the topic, I could see how strongly he felt about it, though both of us did differ on the best way to accomplish the goals. "Songs like that, or anything that carries that powerful a message, could have a strong influence. It's all about finding a way to get the message out and educate people. Entertainment and art is a great way to do that." He shook his head. Wondering why, I said, "But you agree with the message."

This was where Brian got worked up. He was of the opinion that art was only speaking to the already converted. When I asked about his solution, the first word he said was, "Violence." His eyes opened wide. He became louder as he made a passionate argument for a violent revolution. He even argued that the deaths of the oppressors was a good thing. I watched him with fascination. His sudden rant had taken me off guard, so I am sure I looked surprised. Certainly some of what he was saying was hyperbole, otherwise he was a little bit crazy, but that didn't bother me.

Personally, I saw no place for violence in a civil rights movement, but I loved his passion and wanted him to continue. I was about to challenge his violence stance to see if he genuinely thought it through and believed it the best way to go, but out of the blue he changed the subject.

"What are you going to do when you leave town?" Brian asked me.

"I think I want to go to school," I told him. I don't know why I said "I think," since I was now quite certain.

"Go to school?" he asked. "For what?"

"I want to become a veterinarian." He was quiet for a moment. He opened his mouth to say something and then stopped himself. I could tell my revelation had caught him off guard. "What's wrong? Can't a woman have a career?" I smiled.

"Of course you can. You just—I wasn't expecting that. Most women just want a husband and a family. And there's your…" He trailed off, but I knew what he was going to say.

I asked anyway. "My what?"

"Well, um, you know." It was cute the way he squirmed, even if what he was trying to say was insulting. "Your job," he finally said.

"A stripper can't go to college?" I asked, having fun making him squirm at this point.

"It's just not normally done."

"So, you don't think I can do it?"

The uneasiness in him ceased. He took a hold of my hand and looked me in the eye. "I know you can do it."

I could tell he was being sincere. Even though he really didn't know me, it felt good to hear.

"What about you?" I asked. "Do you plan on settling down here?"

"Oh, no. I want more."

"Such as?"

"A bigger career. I'm here for the job. I get to work as a newspaper reporter. But there's more important news out there than Miss O'Leary's cow running amuck through the middle of town. I want to move on to a large paper and cover more important stories: Crime, politics— on a larger scale, then take a stab at writing books."

"So this murder was the perfect thing for you?"

"Oh ye—" He cut himself off as he realized he was

talking to a friend of the victim. "I mean, um—" He looked awfully sorry.

"Don't worry about it," I assured him. "I know what you mean."

He smiled. We then both sat quietly and finished the food in front of us.

After we ate, we went outside and walked together. The sun had set and the temperature had dropped since we had arrived in town. It was now so cold I could see our breath, but it didn't bother me. I was just happy to be with him and enjoying myself.

"There's a tunnel under that building across the street that used to be part of the Underground Railroad," he told me. As we passed the cute little popcorn shop he was referring to he added, "They hid the slaves in a large cave like space under the building."

Brian took me to a spot where a river passed under the main street. We stopped and stood over the waterfall. It felt nice being there with him and listening to the rushing water. I wish it hadn't taken him so long to put his arm around me. I knew that soon I would be gone and would probably never see him again, but that didn't matter now. All that mattered was tonight. I was happy. Tonight was special.

Chapter 32

Bill Harris:

It was late afternoon an' tensions was runnin' high. We all was fuckin' sick o' bein' here an' wanted to git goin'.

Everyone was scared an' cranky. I walked to a group o' carnies who was listenin' to Gino talk. He was talkin' 'bout the murder—said he knew who done it.

"Now Gino," I said, "I don't want you gettin' everyone all riled up, you hear?"

"No, no," he said. "This ain't no game. I know who did it."

"How?" I asked.

"Well, you see, it's like this," he began. "We all know where each other was on the night of the murder. I've been over it. Everyone who could have had any motive has at least one person who knows where they were. Everyone except one person.”

I didn’ know if what he was sayin’ was true, but I knew he was talkin’ ’bout Otto. I should have shut Gino down right there, but I didn’.

“Well, we know that Radowski has no alibi. Now, I don’t know how many of you know this, but ’cause I run the kootch show and spend more time around these broads than anyone, I see things. Otto spent a lot of time around Mary. Followed her around. Was nice to her. He had it bad for old Busty, I tell you.”

Others in the crowd spoke up to confirm this. I had to concede the point. Otto had a thing fer her, we had all seen it.

“Now,” Gino continued. “What do we really know about the man? He doesn’t like to talk about his past. Bill,” he said to me, “what do you know about it?”

I knew Otto had been in some trouble in the past, but I didn’ see no need werkin’ up the crowd. “I don’t know nothin’,” I said.

That’s when the crowd began to talk, people sayin’ what they thought they knew ’bout Radowski’s past, so I came clean. Had to. Their comments ranged from diddlin’ young boys to child murder.

“Quiet. Everyone, listen,” I said to ’em all. “Nothin’ was proven against Otto.” I didn’ remember all the details, but I remembered that.

This didn' stop 'em from talkin' 'bout what Otto might have done.

I tried to calm the crowd. They was gittin' shit ugly. "This is what the cops are fer," I told 'em.

They did not want to hear this. They was sick o' the cops. We all were. We wanted to go home.

They was right 'bout one thing. It sure seemed the cops weren't spendin' enough time talkin' to the old man. We all suspected him, every one o' us. I know he was the first person to pop into my head. Gino led us over to Radowski's trailer to question him. I told Gino not to do anythin' rash, but I reckoned talkin' was okay. If he confessed, we could turn him over to the police an' all go home.

There was 'bout ten people when I first came over to Gino. Now most all o' the carnies were here. Gino knocked on the door.

Otto answered. "Oh, oh, hiya, all."

"Radowski," Gino said firmly, "we want to talk to you."

"Uh, oh, yeah, all righty. About?"

"The murder."

"Oh?" Otto grew pale.

Gino was right 'bout him. I could tell, we all could, from the look in his eyes.

"It very sad," Otto said.

"Otto," Gino said, "we know you had a thing for Mary."

"Yessum, me like her very much. Very good friend to Otto."

"And you saw her that night."

"Yes. She asked me to watch Roscoe. He still here now."

"And you went in her trailer with her."

"No, no. I didn't. No."

"Radowski, don't lie. You were seen going in."

"Oh?"

"So you admit it?"

"No. Don't know. I don't remember going in. Seems like something I wouldn't forget."

Screams o' "He's lying" came from the angry crowd.

I stepped up to Gino an' Otto. "Otto," I said, "listen, I know you didn' plan on this. Jus' tell us the truth an' I'll protect you an' turn you over safely to the cops."

"I don't know nothing," Otto claimed.

"Don't you see what's goin' on here? These people want blood. They want revenge. But mostly, they want this to be over with so they can go home. Why don't you let me take 'em home?"

A tear ran down Otto's face. "I don't know nothing, I swears it," he screamed to the crowd o' his former friends.

It was too late. They were convinced. Suddenly they pushed forward an' took hold o' old Bozo an' carried him off. I wanted to stop it but I was helpless. His fate had been decided an' there was nothin' I could do 'bout it, not against this werked up crowd. I didn' want to watch but I couldn' take my eyes off it. It was painful to see. He kicked, screamed, an' cried, but it did no good. I knew he was guilty an' gittin' what he deserved, but I still felt sorry fer him. I ain't never heard anyone cry like that. It was sickenin'.

Chapter 33

Otto Radowski:

The people here, my friends, thought I done wrong, thought I commit the murder. I know not why, but they did. Made Otto nervous and feel bad. I found it best just to avoid everyone. That made me sad. I loved these people. I loved my job and I loved being here. I never wanted it to end. Just wanted things to go back to like they was. I hoped maybe next year people would forget they suspected Otto, and it could go back being like it was. That hope helped me survive. But I knew it wouldn't go back that night. For the second night in a row, Otto found it best to stay in my trailer a much as I could.

It was night and I was watching a spider build his web in the corner. He was a small guy with black spots.

He didn't seem bothered by me watching so I did. It was nice to have someone who wasn't avoiding poor Otto, since even the cat stayed away from me. I wondered what that spider thought as he built the web.

"What are you thinking, little spider? Hoping to catch some good eats?"

Otto's good feeling was broken when I heard a commotion outside. I didn't know what and didn't want to. It did not concern Otto until the crowd came to my trailer. They were right outside.

I jumped when I hear the knock at Otto's door. What a fright. I felt uneasy, but answered. "Oh," I said when I saw Gino at my door with all my friends behind him. They didn't look like they came for a friendly visit. Otto's heart sank. "Oh," I said, struggling for words. "Hiya, all." I tried to smile. Tried not to assume worst.

"Radowski, we want to talk to you," Gino said.

"Uh…" I didn't know what to say or do, but slowly spit out. "Oh, yeah, all righty." Then I asked "'About?" Otto knew the answer.

"The murder."

Even though I knew he'd say that, the answer still stunned me, yes it did. Why were they picking on poor Otto? "Oh?" I responded. I was sweating and felt the blood leave my face. "It very sad," I told him.

"Otto," Gino said to me, "we know you had a thing for Mary."

I did. It was true. She was nice to old Otto. She was

beautiful inside and out. A sweet soul. You could just tell by the way she loved and cared for that cat of hers. He missed his mummy, that pussy did.

"Yessum," I admitted, "me like her very much. Very good friend to Otto."

"And you saw her that night."

"Yes. She asked me to watch Roscoe. He still here now."

"And you went in her trailer with her."

"No, no. I didn't. No."

"Radowski, don't lie. You were seen going in."

"Oh?" How could that be? I thought for a moment. Tried to remember what they could have seen and if I seen anyone around then.

"So you admit it?"

"No. Don't know. I don't remember going in. Seems like something I wouldn't forget."

Oh but they not believe me. The crowd became loud and angry. I so scared.

Bill came up. Bill always been good friend to Otto. "Otto," he said, "listen, I know you didn' plan on this. Jus' tell us the truth an' I'll protect you an' turn you over safely to the cops."

Oh no, not Bill too. I so sad that he turned on me. My heart broke.

"I don't know nothing." My voice cracked as I said it. Otto so scared. Don't know what they planned. Would I die? Would it hurt?

"Don't you see what's goin' on here?" Bill asked. "These people want blood. They want revenge. But mostly, they want this to be over with so they can go home. Why don't you let me take 'em home?"

Why did Bill want to hurt me? I felt my eyes tear up. So scared. "I don't know nothing, I swears it."

Suddenly the crowd lunged toward me. A mass of angry people. My friends no more. All hate Otto. They grabbed at me. I kicked and screamed and tried to pull away, but it did no good. Otto helpless. They took hold of me and carried me away. Why didn't they believe me? I wanted the police. They'd investigate and see I did nothing wrong.

I cried and pleaded for someone to help me, but no one would.

I tried to be a man but couldn't stop the crying. Otto scared. I hurt inside. I didn't like friends turning on me. Not want to die, least of all like this, with everybody hating me and thinking I done wrong, done something horrible.

"Stop, please!" I screamed.

It all happened so quick. I don't know where they got the rope from but soon it was around my neck and thrown over a tree limb. I pleaded but they wouldn't let me talk. I so frightened. I wanted more time, maybe be arrested, then investigation finds the truth. But it was not to be.

They pulled the rope. As it lifted me off the ground, I lost my air. So much pain. I tried to inhale but could not.

Oh, it hurt like nothing I ever felt ever. I couldn't breathe. I was choking as they was cheering. Cheering! I couldn't even cry as the rope stole my breath. I wanted—

Chapter 34

Bill Harris:

As the crowd slowly left, I just stood there, frozen. Radowski's body was hangin' from a rope, rockin' back an' forth. I hurt inside. Guilty as I knew he was, this should not have happened. It didn' feel like justice. It weren't right. If only Gino hadn' werked everyone up in such a frenzy. Why would he do such a thing? Why not let the law do the job? The police would have gotten Otto. Er maybe not. They hadn' yit. Aw, fuck, I dunno. It was frustratin'. I just know this was bad, very bad. What Gino an' 'em done was forever. There was no erasin' it.

I didn' know what would happen to any o' us after this, but we couldn' all return next year. Not this group. Not together.

These people would be a constant reminder o' when shit went bad here in Ohio.

Maybe this was it fer me—time to retire an' sell out. I had considered sellin' before this, but deep down knew I never actually would. I had this here carnival fer so long an' werked with others before that. It's the only life I knows. But after this, aw shit, it just changed things. It would still be hard to let it go, but it could never be the same. Not after tonight. Not ever.

As I walked away, I could hear the faint creakin' o' the rope.

I went to the telephone an' called the police. I jus' told the man who answered, "Otto Radowski is dead. Someone needs to come to the fairgrounds," an' hung up.

I weren't in no mood fer talkin'. I walked around near the entrance fer a bit. There was a car in the parkin' lot, but it was so dark, an' the car was just far enough away from me that I could not tell who was in it. I was 'bout to sit down when I heard the sirens. Suddenly two police cars, sirens blarin', arrived. As they stopped that reporter an' Arianna exited the car that had been parked. Chief Davis got out o' one o' the cop cars an' his deputy got out o' the other. Davis quickly spoke with the reporter, then came up to me.

"This way," I said.

No other words were said as I walked to the scene, which was at the far edge o' the backyard. I stopped when we reached the last o' the trailers. The body could be seen from there an' I didn' want to go any farther. I turned away as he an' his deputy continued on.

I didn' look in their direction. I didn' want to see Otto again. His screams still rang in my ears. As I thought o' what had happened, I came close to tears, but before that happened I heard footsteps approachin' me from behind. I turned an' saw Chief Davis.

"I tried to stop this from happenin', but it had turned into a mob an' nobody would listen to reason," I said to him.

"Who instigated it?" he asked.

I was still numb. "What do you mean?" I knew what he meant, but I was stallin'.

"Who led the mob?"

"It was—" I stopped. I didn' know wha' to do. I knew what Gino done wasn't right, but his intentions weren't wrong. He wanted justice an' to git rid o' who he thought was the murderer. All those involved did. An' they all wanted to go home. I couldn' turn on 'em fer that, not now anyway. I needed time to think. "It was a group thing," I said. "I don't want to name names."

"I have to find out who is responsible."

I looked down. I wasn' ready to talk 'bout it.

"Who put the rope around Radowski's neck?"

"I can't say," I mumbled.

"That's all for now. Don't leave."

I thought he'd be back, but he later left the fairgrounds without talkin' to me again. I don't know why I couldn' tell him anythin' when he first asked. Maybe I was still in shock. By the time he was gone, I regretted not tellin' him, but still, I didn' call him when I was thinkin' that either. I didn' know what I should do.

Chapter 35

Mary Fontaine,
Saturday, October 31, 1953:

I had been ready to get out of there all night. Some people don't believe this, but I liked my job. Maybe taking my clothes off for strangers isn't what some would call respectable. I didn't care. It's much better than some things I've had to do. I liked the attention, and I liked getting the marks hot. It made me happy knowing that they'd be thinking of me later when they had sex with their girlfriend or wife or when they were all alone. I felt powerful. They thought of me when they left and I thought of them.

I always got a great thrill from sex. My job only enhanced that. But lately the shows just weren't doing it for me. The thrill wasn't there anymore and the memories didn't help me when I was alone. I needed more. I needed excitement. I began experimenting with suffocation and pain. I started mildly, pricking myself with a pin during self-pleasure. Soon I moved on to choking myself with a rope. I knew it was dangerous and I always was careful.

Next, I moved to poking myself with a knife—not enough to draw blood, just enough to feel pain. To feel the pain and the pleasure that went with it. The risks did worry me. I almost had a serious accident when my cat Roscoe tried to jump on me during a session. But the danger didn't stop me. When my mind fixated on pleasure, it was as if I lost all control. I just wanted to make it happen. I wanted to push myself to the limit. Once I decided what I wanted to do, I became obsessed with it until I had my release. There was no stopping me. I may have had an occasional moment of sanity when I realized I needed to stop, but this was always after some dangerous act. Anyway, these thoughts were quickly dismissed the next time my desires were high. The want of pleasure was too great.

And now it was the end of the season. I was worn out after a long year. I needed to relax. I'd been thinking about a new position all day. I had just finished a performance and had some time before my last show. I rushed to my trailer. I thought I'd get all hot, then really enjoy my final show of the year. I saw Otto on the way. I asked him to watch my cat for a while. He came to my door with me. I went inside to get Roscoe. He looked up at me.

He was sitting on my bed. I picked him up and the cute kitty began to purr. I loved it when he purred. I hugged him. "I love you so much," I said. I told him, "Mommy's going to let Otto watch you for a bit. I'll come get you and bring you home soon, honey."

I went back outside. Roscoe clung to me but didn't put up a fight when I gave him to Otto. I said a quick thanks and closed my door. It was good to get rid of him for the moment. This way I wouldn't have to worry about any unexpected surprises. I was now ready for fun.

It felt good to finally be alone. I was already sexually aroused and felt goose bumps when I pulled out the butcher knife. It looked so sharp and deadly that I squirmed with pleasure. I touched the point of the long, shiny silver, sexy knife. Ouch, it was sharp. Oh, I was ready to go. I quickly stripped off what little I had on.

I lay back and began touching myself. Oh, it felt so good to finally be doing it. I moaned. It was so satisfying. I only did this for a few moments, I was too excited to wait any longer. I got on my knees on the bed. As I leaned forward, I held the handle of the knife down on the bed in front of me. The knife was pointing straight up. I shivered with anticipation. I slowly brought my body forward until the tip of the knife made contact with my neck.

Chills ran up my thighs as I felt the cold steel poke me. I held the knife and leaned on my elbow to hold myself up. Then I moved my hand so the only thing holding the knife in place was the pressure from my neck. The sharp tip felt so good. I reached down with my other hand and began to touch myself.

All of my cares and frustrations were gone. It felt amazing. For the moment, all I knew was extreme pleasure. The prick of the knife pushing into my throat as my fingertips, running in circles, brought me closer and closer. I was so worked up from thinking about this all day, and from the steel pressing into my neck, that it didn't take long. As I reached climax, I lost the power to hold myself up.

Chapter 36

Tom Davis,
Thursday, November 5, 1953:

When Paul and I arrived at the fairgrounds, Bill met us at the gate. Somehow, that goddamned reporter was already there. He came right up to me. "Brian, get away from here now," I told him. I didn't have any time for him now.

"What happened?"

"I can't deal with you now. If you enter the fairgrounds, I will have you arrested." Then I turned to Bill. "So?"

"This way," he said somberly and led us to Radowski's body.

Bill stayed back as Paul and I approached the victim. He was hanging from a tree limb on the back edge of the yard where the carnies had been living. The body was perfectly still on this cool, quiet, and windless night.

I told Paul, "Guard the body until Detective Perry and the others from county arrive. Don't let anyone near it for any reason." Then I walked back to Bill and talked with him.

"I tried to stop this from happenin', but it had turned into a mob and nobody would listen to reason," he told me. He was clearly troubled by what had happened.

"Who instigated it?" I asked.

"What do you mean?"

"Who led the mob?"

"It was—" He paused. "It was a group thing. I don't want to name names."

"I have to find out who is responsible."

He looked at the ground.

"Who put the rope around Radowski's neck?" I asked.

"I can't say," he muttered, barely audible.

I considered taking him down to the station to question him but soon decided against it. He was obviously shaken by the events of the past week, and I didn't want to put him through any more unpleasantness.

I planned to get the needed information from him— just not at that moment. "That's all for now," I told him. "Don't leave."

I walked up to the next person I saw, which was Betty Bates. "Excuse me, Miss Bates."

"Not more of this." She looked more than disappointed to see me. It was a beaten-down look.

"Excuse me?" I asked.

"Do we have to sit around for another week while you investigate who killed Otto? Can't we just go before more die?" She walked away.

I questioned others and none of them were willing to name names. These people wanted nothing to do with me, which was understandable. They believed they had lynched the man responsible for Mary's death and didn't want anyone punished for administering "justice." As crazy as this was, a small part of me thought they were right. What good would come from pushing an investigation into the lynching? It wasn't like I would be taking dangerous persons off of the streets. None of them were likely to do this again. It was the moment. They were all caught up in the storm and Radowski's death happened. It was that simple.

But I knew I could not let it end there. The lynching may have been largely the result of mass hysteria, but some person or persons led it. They may very well have lynched a guilty man, but that is for a court of law to decide, not them. We all know from history that if we allow this kind of justice, the innocent as well as the guilty will suffer. Still, so far none of those who witnessed or were involved in this event wanted to talk.

Most of them weren't guilty of anything except obstructing justice, so I decided to take a different approach to the lynching than I had to the previous murder. These people had been kept here long enough for the one crime, and I didn't feel right about keeping them any longer because of the new crime, committed by probably only a few. I decided to let them go home. I'd give them some time—maybe a week—then I'd travel around to their homes and question them. I thought that probably a number of them, after having some time to reflect and some distance from the other carnies, would realize it was best to tell the truth about what happened and do so without the threat of incarceration.

I went back to the crime scene, where the people from county were now working. It was the same group of four that were here after the last murder. Lori Kirk was photographing the body as I approached.

"Hey," I said to detective Perry. "What do you think?"

"It's a lynching. Did anyone tell you anything?"

"Not a thing. No one wants anything to do with me."

"I'm not surprised," he responded, then, after a pause, he said, "There's nothing for me to do here. Once they finish collecting the evidence, I'm done with this one. It'll be all about witnesses. Take care of it. Dolan doesn't want me wasting time on another dead carnival person. I don't give a shit about a dead killer clown anyway." He gave me a big smile, as if he meant that last statement to be humorous. He really was an uncaring asshole.

Seriously, I said, "I'll take care of it."

I turned to my deputy-chief. "Stay here until they are done," I told him. "After that, find Bill Harris and let him know the carnies are free to leave."

As for the reason they had been kept here, this would be the end of it. I thought this over as I returned to my car. I had not only been making no progress with the investigation, but there didn't seem to be anything left to be found. Although the thought did cross my mind that if anyone knew anything important that they were hiding from me, when they were next interviewed in their homes and away from the others, they might decide to talk. This was possible—so I kept a little hope—but very doubtful. It was time for me to deal with that cold reality that I would likely never solve this case. I rethought the decision as I drove back to the station. By the time I arrived, I was confident I was handling this the right way. I sat at my desk and leaned back.

My thoughts turned to Radowski and Fontaine. This had begun with the cold-blooded murder of poor Mary Fontaine, and she wasn't coming back. If the murderer was now dead, that was a good thing. I'll admit I had my doubts about Otto Radowski's guilt, but he was as good a suspect as any. The truth is I didn't have any evidence linking him or anyone else to the crime. If someone else did it, I wasn't going to locate them. It was that simple. If it wasn't Radowski, then the murderer got away with it. While deep down I knew that nothing I could do would prevent that, and nothing good would come from pursuing this any further, I wasn't ready to close the case just yet. Soon the suspects and potential witnesses would all be home, and I would be questioning them again in regards to Radowski's murder. While doing so, I'd work in a few casual questions about the Fontaine murder. Maybe then, with separation of time and space, someone would reconsider telling me something they previously held back. It wasn't likely, but at this point it was all I had. Publically, I'd say the case was closed, hoping then the guilty party would let their guard down. It was the last chance to learn the truth.

The sun was beginning to rise as I filed the case paperwork. It was then that that reporter came into the station.

"So, what happened?" he asked, with his notebook out and ready.

I knew I had to be careful about what I told him. I did not want the town's folks thinking the wrong man had been lynched and the murderer was still on the loose.

"Otto Radowski was lynched—hanged from a tree. In the eyes of those who did it, it was justice for the Fontaine murder."

"Who is responsible?"

"I don't know."

"You investigated it, didn't you?"

"No one would talk. They all refused to tell me anything."

"Then aren't they all guilty of obstructing justice?"

"What am I going to do?"

I did not want it getting into the papers that the carnies would be questioned at their homes. I didn't want them expecting it. I knew there would be a negative public reaction to the impression that I was dropping this, but right then I decided that no matter what the reaction was, I would wait it out. People would eventually learn that I bluffed about dropping the lynching, and then what they thought before would not matter, so I told Stockton, "I'm not going to arrest them all. They're not bad people, some just snapped. It will be impossible to find out who instigated the lynching without a witness talking, which all of them refused to do."

"So you're not going to do anything?"

I had to be careful how I answered this. If I said no, it would appear that I condoned the lynching, however I didn't want to give the carnies a heads up that they'd be questioned about this, and soon. The best I could come up with was, "I have no comment."

He shook his head after I said this. "If you say so," he responded. "So, where are you with the Fontaine murder investigation?"

I thought it was best to keep my answer simple and let everyone believe that Fontaine's murderer was dead. "That ends the investigation into the Mary Fontaine murder," I told him.

"Ends it? How?"

"The probable killer is dead. Case closed."

Chapter 37

Brian Stockton,
Friday, November 6, 1953:

I didn't sleep that night. Davis didn't want me at the fairgrounds, which was understandable since, as I soon found out, Radowski was just hanged from a tree. Arianna had stood back and watched my conversation with Davis.

After I spoke with Davis, I went back to Arianna, who told me, "I have to go check on my friends and find out what happened."

It was obvious something bad had transpired while we were gone. Sympathetically, I told Arianna, "Go do what you need to."

She kissed me on the cheek and ran off.

Even though I had just been told not to enter the fairgrounds, I needed to learn what I could, so I snuck around to try to get interviews and just made sure Davis never saw me.

I approached a small group of people. I went up to the stripper Amy. "Excuse me. Can you tell me what happened here?"

"Go to hell," she snapped. The carnies with her all glared at me.

I turned to the kootch show operator, who was near. Before I spoke he told me to "Fuck off."

This was everyone's attitude. I failed in every attempt to learn anything at all. Nobody wanted anything to do with me, and they were all quick to tell me where I could go. When I saw Radowski's body, I knew what had happened. I thought about finding Arianna, since she might have learned more details from her friends, but I decided against it. We had just had a wonderful time out and that was what I wanted to remember, not me trying to get her to snitch on her friends. This meant I may have missed some of the story, but so be it.

I went to the office and wrote up a small blurb just to say that a carny, Otto Radowski, was killed last night and that details were not known. After that I took a walk through town and then sat for a while by the waterfall to pass the night.

Early the next morning, I walked to the police station to see Chief Davis. It was still dark outside when I entered the station. "So, what happened?" I asked him.

"Otto Radowski was lynched—hanged from a tree," he told me. "In the eyes of those who did it, it was justice for the Fontaine murder."

"Who is responsible?"

"I don't know."

"You investigated it, didn't you?"

"No one would talk. They all refused to tell me anything." That wasn't surprising. I had the same reaction from the people I tried speaking to. But I didn't have the authority he did.

I asked him, "Then aren't they all guilty of obstructing justice?"

"What am I going to do? I'm not going to arrest them all. They're not bad people, some just snapped. It will be impossible to find out who instigated the lynching without a witness talking, which all of them refused to do."

"So you're not going to do anything?" I knew that couldn't be right.

He was silent for a few seconds. "I have no comment."

What a ridiculous answer. "If you say so. So, where are you with the Fontaine murder investigation?"

"That ends the investigation into the Mary Fontaine murder."

"Ends it? How?" I was shocked.

"The probable killer is dead. Case closed."

I felt like he had to be joking, even though I knew he wasn't. Unless all the evidence pointed to Radowski and the only reason Davis hadn't arrested him yet was because he was trying to get more evidence to secure a conviction, I couldn't understand how the lynching of a suspect ended the investigation. Nothing else was said between us. With that information, I left him.

So that was it? The lynching of Otto Radowski officially closed the case? This didn't seem right. I returned to the fairgrounds. A few people were out but again no one wanted to speak with me. It was then that a police car pulled up. It was Paul Inzalaco. I met him at the entrance. "Paul, what are you doing here?"

"Um, I'm here to inform them that they are free to leave."

I nodded and he walked on. Free to leave? What was Davis doing? It seemed like he suddenly gave up. It was as if the lynching had broken his spirits. It was frustrating to see.

I walked through the fairgrounds one last time. I didn't see anyone out who hadn't shot me down until I saw her. It was Arianna. She was sitting on the steps of the merry-go-round. I walked up to her.

I said, "Hi."

She looked up and tried to smile. Her eyes were red from crying. "Hey," she quietly said.

"I'm sorry to see you like this."

"I'm sorry for Otto. That poor man." Tears were running down her cheeks. "He was such a sweet person."

"Do you know who…you know?" I asked.

"No. No one wants to talk about it. This is just awful. I—" She paused then said, "Well, it will come out."

"Maybe, maybe not."

"What do you mean? With that many witnesses, they have to…" She trailed off.

"That's if Chief Davis pursues this."

"How can he not?" She became louder. "A man is dead."

"I honestly don't know, but I just visited him and he didn't seem too interested in taking this any further." She looked at me in disbelief. I shared her shock and frustration. "I've heard he's letting you all go home."

"What?" She stood up. "That can't be." Her voice was a mixture of anger and sadness. "I mean, I want to leave, but that man keeps us here, it leads to another murder, and now he just forgets it all? No investigation? That can't be true. We can't be leaving now."

I put my hand on her shoulder. "It's what I've been told." I felt sick telling her this.

It was then that Bill came by shouting over and over, "Everybody pack up. We're leavin'."

Arianna looked at him and then back at me with fresh tears running down her face. "I can't—" she said just above a whisper. She stopped then said, "I don't know what to do."

I couldn't imagine what she felt, but I gave her the best advice I could. "Go home," I told her. "Put this behind you."

"But what about Otto?"

"What can you do about that?"

"Put pressure on the chief. Public awareness. Protest."

"I'm a reporter, Arianna. I can do that."

We stood for perhaps a minute not saying anything.

"I guess I should prepare to leave Arianna finally said in an exhausted sounding voice. "Do promise you won't let this drop?"

"I promise."

"Well, I suppose I…" She trailed off.

"I understand." I took out my notepad and a pencil and wrote down my address and phone number. I ripped it off and handed it to her. "If you're ever lonely, or just want to talk."

She looked at it and smiled. "Until we meet again," she said and gave me a light kiss on the lips.

"Until we meet again," I said and watched her walk out of my life. Then I left.

That day I wrote about the lynching of Otto Radowski and about the decision of Chief Davis to let the carnies leave town. The next day it was the headline in the local paper and my write-up also made the front page, above the fold, in Cleveland. Over the next few days, I found that everyone in town seemed to feel the same way as Davis—that the Radowski lynching closed the case. There were some doubts about Radowski's guilt, but since everyone believed that Radowski was probably guilty of the murder, I supposed they thought it was best to just accept it as fact. Everybody was clearly ready to move on. However, outside of town people felt differently.

Davis's decision immediately received statewide and regional coverage. Editorials from Toledo to Pittsburgh to Columbus slammed his decision and "Chief Lynch," a term I used to describe him in the headline of an editorial I had written for the Cleveland paper a day after the lynching, was now how he was publicly known.

The county sheriff quickly stepped in. He immediately came to town and met with the mayor and city council. At his urging—it probably didn't take much—they relieved Davis of his duties. A source at the police station told me that Davis didn't even get a chance to explain himself. He was called by the mayor and told to clean out his desk. The mayor hung up before Davis could say a word. With the publicity they were receiving, this didn't surprise me.

Mayor Johnson had to be embarrassed at the press the lynching brought the town. The mayor and sheriff held a short press conference to announce this decision and to let it be known that lynch law would not be tolerated. Mayor Johnson spoke first. He apologized for all that had gone on then stated, "But now is the time to look forward. After meeting with Sheriff Dolan and the City Council this morning, I informed Chief Thomas Davis that he has been removed from office. He will no longer be with the police department in any capacity. Deputy-Chief Paul Inzalaco has been promoted to Chief of Police. I expect him to bring honor and dignity back to the office. For more details on the investigation, I'll let Sheriff Dolan take over." The mayor stepped aside and Dolan took his place in front of the podium.

"I'd like to begin with an apology to your town and, most off all, to the victims of these two horrible crimes," Sheriff Dolan stated. "I apologize for not keeping a closer watch on Chief Davis. I had been in constant contact with Davis in the week following the murder of Fontaine and just after the lynching of Radowski and was assured by him that he had everything under control. This was obviously not the case. I take full responsibility for not keeping a closer watch on what he was doing. Like Mayor Johnson said, now is the time to look forward. I'm here to announce that a detective from my office, Patrick Perry, will take over the lynching investigation. He's a smart, experienced, and compassionate detective. There isn't a better man for the job. I'd like to introduce Detective Perry."

Perry then took the podium. "It is with great sadness and determination that I stand before you. Sadness because of the terrible crime that has taken place and at the pathetic response from local law enforcement, and determination to bring about justice. Let me be clear, visitors to this great county of ours are to be treated as one of us. I find it sickening that a member of law enforcement, someone who had risen to the ranks of chief, no less, could think that these murders could be just brushed aside because the victims were outsiders. That makes them guests, and that is not how guests deserve to be treated. I'm not going to give details of the investigation I have planned, but let me assure you, justice will be done, and be done quickly. Thank you."

Perry stepped away from the podium. Neither he nor Sheriff Dolan took questions.

Pat Perry proved to be true to his word. Immediately after speaking, Perry headed to the airport. He went to Florida, where several of the carnies lived. Two days after the press conference, Gino Guglielmo was arrested in Florida, charged with the murder of Otto Radowski.

The magazine editor who contacted me shortly after the first murder now offered me the chance to write up this story for his national publication. I wrote a long piece about the murders and the investigation, intertwined with my experience covering the story. It included everything from my night reviewing the carnival to Gugleilmo's arrest. From there the story spread. The lynching and events that followed went from a regional to a national story. Detective Perry became a hero and "Chief Lynch" went into hiding.

With that, it was time for me to move on. The exposure I received from the article brought me numerous job offers. I took a job in San Francisco. I would finally be a real journalist, reporting for a real magazine. I was also weighing offers to write a book about the case. This was my break, and I intended to capitalize on it.

I felt bad about losing contact with Arianna. She was a lovely and intelligent girl. I had no way to contact her to tell her I was moving and didn't leave a forwarding address because this was a good chance to separate from people I had been trying to avoid. Arianna was a regrettable casualty of this. It was probably for the best, though, I thought. She had her life and I had mine. We would always have that night together. I would remember it, and her, fondly.

It was with great expectations that I walked out to my packed-up Chevy to begin a new phase of my life. Before leaving, I drove into town, parked, and stood next to my car. I lit a cigarette and took in the town one last time as I mentally said goodbye. Then I entered my car and began my journey west. As I drove out of town, I took the final drag off my cigarette.

About the Author

Corey Recko's first book, *Murder on the White Sands: The Disappearance of Albert and Henry Fountain*, won the Wild West History Association's award for the "Best Book on Wild West History" for 2007. *New Mexico Magazine* said of the book, "The story moves along like detective fiction…" Of his second book, *A Spy for the Union: The Life and Execution of Timothy Webster*, the *Civil War News* review of the book concluded, "Just about everyone will find something to like in this tale of Civil War espionage that mixes in portions of heroism, intrigue, cowardice, and betrayal." Along with books, Recko has written articles on a variety of historical topics for magazines and historical journals and has become a sought-after speaker (including an appearance on C-SPAN). *Death of a Kootch Show Girl*, a mystery about a death at a small-town carnival in 1953, is Recko's first novel.

www.ingramcontent.com/pod-product-compliance
Lightning Source LLC
Chambersburg PA
CBHW070426120726
47910CB00003B/661